THUNDER RANGE

Jackson Cole

Chivers Press · G.K. Hall & Co.
Bath, England · Thorndike, Maine USA

This Large Print edition is published by Chivers Press, England, and by G.K. Hall & Co., USA.

Published in 1998 in the U.K. by arrangement with Golden West Literary Agency.

Published in 1998 in the U.S. by arrangement with Golden West Literary Agency.

U.K. Hardcover   ISBN 0–7540–3435–6 (Chivers Large Print)
U.K. Softcover   ISBN 0–7540–3436–4 (Camden Large Print)
U.S. Softcover   ISBN 0–7838–0244–7 (Nightingale Series Edition)

An earlier version of this story appeared as "Riders of the Dead Star Trail" by Jackson Cole in *Texas Rangers* (7/48).

The text of this Large Print edition is unabridged.
Other aspects of the book may vary from the original edition.

Set in 16 pt. New Times Roman.

Printed in Great Britain on acid-free paper.

British Library Cataloguing in Publication Data available

Library of Congress Cataloging-in-Publication Data

Cole, Jackson.
    Thunder range : a Jim Hatfield Texas Ranger western / by Jackson Cole.
        p. cm.
    ISBN 0–7838–0244–7 (lg. print : sc : alk. paper)
    1. Large type books.   I. Title.
[PS3505.O2685T5   1998]
813'.54—dc21   98–21236

CHAPTER ONE

'Goldy, this is the darndest snake track I ever rode. I'm about ready to believe that old yarn about how it came to be. It sure looks as if it was burned out by something red-hot rolling down through the hills.'

With a disgusted oath, Jim Hatfield pulled his tall sorrel to a halt, hitched one long leg over the saddle horn, fished the makin's from his shirt pocket and proceeded to roll a cigarette with the slim fingers of his left hand. He lit the brain tablet and glanced back the way he had come. Southward, veering slightly to the west, stretched the ancient trail, a broad ribbon of tarnished silver in the moonlight. Empty, lonely, desolate. Directly ahead, like a vast fortress hewed from a single block of stone, Perdida Mountain glowed in the white fire of the moon.

Hatfield's tall form was powdered with the gray dust of the desert they had just crossed. His broad shoulders sagged a little and he slumped forward in the saddle. His bronzed face was etched with deep lines of fatigue and there were dark circles beneath the long, black-lashed eyes of a peculiar shade of green. His garb—typical rangeland costume—showed the signs of hard and long travel, from dimpled, broad-brimmed 'J.B.' to scuffed boots of softly tanned leather. His plain batwing chaps and faded overalls were scratched and snagged by thorns. So was his open-collar blue shirt. A silken handkerchief of a deeper blue was lopped around his bronzed throat and encircling his sinewy waist were double cartridge belts from which hung carefully worked and oiled holsters that sagged under the weight of heavy black guns.

The magnificent golden horse also seemed on the verge of exhaustion. His head hung low. His glorious black mane rippled dispiritedly as he stumbled over the uneven surface of the sinister trail.

The full moon had crossed the zenith and was pouring a flood of ghostly light down the vast rampart of Perdida's western slope. It silvered the edges of storm clouds that rolled slowly up from the western horizon. On the dark breast of the cloud bank was a flicker of lightning. The air quivered to the mutter of distant thunder.

Hatfield glanced wearily toward the ominous cloud bank. 'Goldy,' he told the horse, 'Along with everything else, it looks like we're in for a good wetting.' He turned his gaze up the mountain slope and his eyes quickened with interest.

Perhaps a hundred yards above the trail was a broad bench well grown with grass, stands of sotol and bristles of thicket. In the face of the beetling cliff beyond was a dark opening. He

2

eyed it speculatively and pulled the big sorrel to a halt.

'Appears to be a cave,' he remarked, 'and from the looks of the grass and stuff, there'd ought to be water. Horse, I've a notion we could do worse than hole up there till the storm's over. You can fill your belly, and I could stand a helpin' of chuck myself, and a mite of shuteye. Still got some coffee, bacon and a few eggs left in the saddlebag. Suppose we take a try at it.'

It was a hard scramble up the slope to the bench, but the golden horse made it without much trouble. In front of the cave his rider dismounted, broke off a dry sotol stalk and touched a match to the splintered end. The sotol burned with a clear flame, providing a very satisfactory torch. Hatfield approached the cave.

'Don't want to den up with a rattlesnake or two,' he explained.

The floor of the cave, however, was clean and dry and there were no signs of reptilian occupancy. A trickle of water flowed along one wall in a shallow channel to lose itself amid the growth outside.

'Couldn't be better,' Hatfield enthused. 'And that rainstorm is coming up fast.'

With swift efficiency he got the rig off the horse. He unrolled a blanket and spread it on the cave floor. Turning the horse loose to graze, he broke off a large quantity of sotol stalks and dead branches in the thickets. Soon he had a good fire going. A little later coffee was bubbling in a little flat bucket, bacon sizzling in a small skillet. He unwrapped several carefully packed and padded eggs and broke them in with the bacon. A small hunch of bread was also forthcoming from the saddlebag. With appreciation he sat down to a savory meal which he consumed by the light of the fire and to the music of the loudening thunder. Goldy cropped contentedly outside the cave in which he would seek shelter when the storm broke.

Meanwhile, Goldy's rider rolled a cigarette and smoked contentedly, while he gazed at the lightning forking and webbing the black sky with pale gold. Finally he pinched out his cigarette butt and tossed it away. From his pocket he drew a smeary scrap of paper upon which was an illiterate-appearing scrawl. Drawing his black brows together, he read the disjointed sentence—

Jim Hatfield stay out of Perdida country. You aint wanted here. Come here and you aint got a chance in an hundred to git out alive. We aint fooling.

Quantrell

Hatfield turned the paper over in his slim fingers, turned it over again and gazed at it with a thoughtful look in his green eyes. It had come

4

to him at Ranger Post headquarters some two weeks before, the day after Captain Bill McDowell had suggested that a little ride over to the Perdida country wouldn't be a bad notion for his ace-man.

''Pears there's a feller operatin' over there,' Captain Bill had said. 'Raisin' hell and shovin' a chunk under a corner. Goes by the name of Quantrell, I understand. Must have took over the name from Quantrell the hell raiser of Civil War days. Of course, Bill Quantrell has been dead years and years—before you were born, Jim, but folks still remember the name.'

'Just like the owlhoot brand,' Hatfield remarked, 'to take the name of some big skookum he-wolf and try to live up to his reputation.'

'From the reports I been gettin', this hellion is doin' a purty good chore of it,' McDowell grunted. 'He's sure got the section set by the ears. Sort of a mysterious jigger nobody has ever seen for sure. Some say he's tall, others say he's short. Sometimes he's reported as wearin' big black whiskers. Other folks swear he's clean shaved. Different folks who have tangled with his outfit tell different stories.'

'Could be more than one of him,' Hatfield observed.

'I've thought of that,' McDowell admitted. 'Let one hellion begin buildin' up a rep'tation and others fall in line and pretend to be him. But each chore that's been pulled over there

5

wears a similarity that sort of marks 'em for the work of one outfit. Of course, different folks may spot different members of the bunch for top worker. But I figger there is some smart and salty jigger directin' operations, all right. Well, you got a hard week of ridin' before you, Jim, and a tough chore at the end of it.'

McDowell paused a moment, then voiced a word of warning.

'And I wouldn't be a bit surprised if you'll be recognized when you show up in the Perdida country,' he said. 'You're gettin' mighty well known all over Texas. The day is past when you can ride into any section as a wanderin' cowhand and get away with it. That devil Quantrell seems to have means of finding out everything that goes on. He's lifted gold shipments and payrolls that were supposed to be plumb secret, and eluded traps set for him as if he'd been told about them in advance. I wouldn't be a mite surprised if he's already figured out that sooner or later I'd send you gunnin' for him. So watch your step. *Adios*, and good luck!'

The very next morning McDowell's shrewd surmise had been justified when Hatfield received the warning scrawl through the mail. He had been about to cast it contemptuously aside when he noted a peculiarity of wording. He decided to keep it, and now he studied it intently by the light of his dying fire.

'Handwriting obviously disguised,' he

mused. 'Nobody who could write at all ever wrote that bad. And one little slip. Not much, but maybe enough to drop a loop around some jigger's neck before the last brand's run.'

Hatfield folded the paper and carefully stowed it in a cunningly contrived secret pocket in his broad leather belt. Then he looked over at Goldy. As is often the case with men who ride much alone, Hatfield had a habit of talking to his horse. Now he addressed the sorrel as he would a fellow traveller.

'You know, feller, being a Texas Ranger is okay, and I wouldn't trade with anybody,' he said, 'but there are times when it's darn hard work. And this is one of them. Well, guess I asked for work when I took over the job. Or, rather, when I agreed to take over.'

He chuckled a little, his eyes dreamy. His tired mind was in a mood for introspection and his thoughts drifted back to the day, quite a few years before, when young Jim Hatfield, fresh from college, sat in the office of Captain Bill McDowell of the Rangers.

The lines in his face were not so deeply etched in those days, but his mouth had a bitter twist to it and his green eyes a hard and feverish glitter. Thinking back, he could almost hear the old Ranger Captain's deep voice.

'Folks tell me you aim to ride on the trail of the wide-loopers who killed your father, Jim?' McDowell said, interrogatively.

'That's right, sir. I aim to even up the score.

7

Poor Dad never had a chance. The hellions shot him in the back. I aim to follow them to hell and back, if necessary.'

'And if you catch up with them?'

'Hand them just what they handed Dad.'

McDowell nodded. 'That's why I called you in to talk to you, Jim,' he said. 'I knew your father before you were born. Sid Hatfield and me were pretty close to each other in the old days. I'd hate to see the son of my old friend riding the outlaw trail.'

'The outlaw trail? What do you mean by that, sir?'

'I mean it's a risky chore you're handing yourself. When a man sets out to take the law in his own hands, he's taking big chances. Sooner or later, there's a good chance that he'll run smack up against the law himself. And all of a sudden find he's in the same class as the hellions he's after.'

'I realize that, sir, but I don't intend to let those devils get away with it.'

'No,' agreed the Captain, 'they mustn't be allowed to get away with it. But I want to help you steer clear of what all too often happens to a man riding the vengeance trail. I'm offering you a job.'

'A job?'

'Yes. With the Texas Rangers. Then you'll be an accredited peace officer, working on the side of the law, with all the power of the State of Texas and organized society to back you up.'

Hatfield's lips twisted. 'A fine use to which to put a college education and a couple of degrees,' he said bitterly. 'Gunning for border scum!'

McDowell did not appear much impressed by the outburst.

'Studied civil engineering in college, didn't you?' he asked.

'Yes.'

'And specialized in geology and petrology, the science of rocks?'

'That's right.'

'Good things to know about in this country,' said McDowell. 'Liable to come in handy, for a Ranger.'

He fixed his cold gray eyes on Hatfield's face.

'Jim,' he said, 'don't get the notion that all a Ranger needs is a fast gun hand. There have been and still are college men in the Rangers. And outlaws are not made up of stupid oafs without brains who only know how to pull a trigger. There are educated, shrewd, able men among the owlhoots. Men who can think as fast as they can shoot. It takes brains and fast thinking to outwit 'em. You'll not be lowering your sights by signing up with the Rangers. And of course, after you run down those killers, you'll be at liberty to leave the service if you want to.'

Hatfield considered, his face somber. Abruptly he made up his mind and voiced the cow country's laconic acceptance of a job.

'Well, sir, I reckon you've hired yourself a hand.'

Jim Hatfield brought his father's killers to justice and saw them die kicking in a noose by due process of law. And as the years passed, he was glad that he had not soiled his own hands with the blood of personal vengeance.

For Jim Hatfield didn't leave the Rangers after his quest ended. The spirit of the finest band of peace officers the world has ever known had gotten into his blood. And now the Lone Wolf, as a stern old Lieutenant of Rangers had dubbed him, was a name known throughout Texas and beyond. Hated and feared by evildoers, honored and respected by honest men!

Hatfield's mind snapped back to the present. He sighed and pinched out his cigarette butt. Then he carefully arranged his blanket, made a pillow of his saddle, and with his guns ready he went to sleep to the accompaniment of rolling thunder and dashing rain. Inside the cave mouth Goldy also slept, but with one eye open and with ears cocked for any unusual sound that might filter through the uproar outside.

It was an unusual sound that aroused Hatfield shortly before dawn. He sat up feeling greatly refreshed. In fact he was a new man in that clean, rain-washed mountain air as he listened to a peculiar creaking and rumbling that drifted up from the trail below.

His fire had died to gray ashes, but the storm had passed and reddish light streamed into the cave mouth from the great globe of the sullen moon that hung just over the western mountain crests.

Hatfield slipped to the mouth of the cave and peered out. He could see the trail clearly outlined in the lurid light, on it a high two-wheeled cart drawn by four sturdy oxen creeping along it. A figure wearing a broad, flopping hat was hunched on the driver's seat. The body of the cart was heaped high with something that gleamed in the moonlight.

'Salt cart headed for Mexico,' the Lone Wolf muttered. 'Been up to the salt lakes to the northeast of here, and bringing back a load.'

He glanced at the moon, the lower edge of which was now touching the western crags, gazed after the cart for a moment and turned back to his blankets. It still wanted almost an hour till dawn.

For better than half an hour, Hatfield dozed, luxuriating in the unwonted pleasure of total relaxation. Goldy also seemed filled with peace and taking his comfort. Suddenly, however, his sensitive ears pricked forward. He blew softly through his nose.

Hatfield opened his eyes, glanced inquiringly toward the horse, now clearly outlined in the strengthening light of dawn. He sat up as the sound that had attracted Goldy's interest reached him. A rhythmical clicking

11

drawing quickly nearer—the sound of swift hoofs beating the hard surface of the trail. He rose to his feet, stepped to the mouth of the cave, but took care to keep well back in the shadow. He gazed toward where the trail curved around the mountain base to the north.

From around the curve bulged a troop of hard riding horsemen, a full dozen of them. Gigantic, unreal in the elusive light, they swept past, drumming toward the desert that was now bathed in a tremulous golden glow.

Hatfield stepped forward and followed their progress with interested eyes. Far out on the desert, two miles or more distant, he could see the salt cart crawling slowly southward. He saw the driver twist about on his seat and gaze at the approaching horsemen. Abruptly he faced to the front and from the movement of his arm, Hatfield judged he was urging his shambling oxen to greater speed. The racing horsemen swiftly closed the distance. Hatfield uttered a sharp exclamation.

A puff of whitish smoke mushroomed from the ranks of the riders. Even before he heard the crack of the distant rifle, Hatfield saw the ox cart driver throw up his arms, pitch sideways from his seat and sprawl motionless on the ground. The oxen stopped, turning their heads to look about. The horsemen charged forward with abated speed.

Up to the cart and the motionless figure they charged, jerking their horses to a halt with such

12

suddenness that the sliding hoofs kicked up little puffs of dust. They dismounted. One strode to the prostrate driver, looked down at him, turned away. The others swarmed over the cart. The salt misted through the air as they scooped it up with their hands and flung it from the heaped-up bed.

With lightning speed, Jim Hatfield got the rig on Goldy. He sent the big sorrel skittering down the slope. As the horse's irons rang on the hard surface, Hatfield's great voice boomed out like a golden bugle call—

'Trail, Goldy, trail!'

Instantly the great sorrel extended himself. His irons drummed the trail, his steely legs shot backward like pistons. He seemed literally to pour his long body over the ground. Mane tossing in the wind of his passing, eyes rolling, nostrils flaring red, he charged toward the group of killers busy with the salt cart.

Suddenly heads were flung up, faces turned toward the speeding horseman. A moment later, puffs of smoke spurted from the cart. Bullets sang past the golden horse and his tall rider.

Face bleak as the granite of Perdida Mountain, eyes the cold gray of a stormy winter sky, Jim Hatfield reached down and slid his heavy Winchester from the boot. He spoke to Goldy, who leveled off to a smooth running walk. Hatfield cuddled the rifle butt against his shoulder. His eyes glanced along the sights. His hand squeezed the stock.

The rifle bucked in his grasp. The report rang out clear and metallic. One of the men on the salt cart went over-board like a hurled sack of old clothes.

Again the rifle boomed. A second man reeled sideways, his arms flopping. Hatfield could almost hear his yell of pain. A third report, and a third man down, clawing and kicking on top of the cart. The others leaped to the ground and fled wildly toward their plunging horses that were being held by three of the group. Without an instant's hesitation they flung themselves into the saddles and went racing away southward, one reeling and swaying in the hull. Behind them they left three motionless figures, instead of one. Hatfield sent shot after shot whining after them. He paused to stuff fresh cartridges into the magazine, speaking to Goldy. The sorrel resumed his racing gallop. Hatfield leaned forward, his eyes intent on the fugitives he was gradually overhauling. Abruptly he muttered an oath.

The edge of the sun was above the eastern horizon, but it was growing darker. Racing out of the east was a long, dark line that swirled and danced, billowing from the surface of the desert to the blue of the darkening sky.

'Sand storm!' the Lone Wolf muttered disgustedly. 'Cutting right across the trail. Those hellions are getting a break.'

14

Even as he spoke, the fleeing horsemen vanished into the wall of dust and sand particles. A few moments later Hatfield pulled Goldy to a halt beside the motionless cart.

A single glance told him there was nothing to be done for the driver. The heavy rifle slug had torn through him from back to chest, just above the heart. Also, there was nothing more to be feared from the two raiders. One lay huddled on the ground, the other sprawled across the salt in the cart.

Hatfield glanced at the darkening sky. He desired to give the scene of the killing a careful going over; but he knew the danger in that ominous dark line that swirled across the desert a scant quarter of a mile to the south. The storm was flowing from east to west in the clearly defined path, but some wind vagary might shift it to the north and engulf him in the blinding clouds of dust and sand.

Perhaps a hundred yards to the north of the cart was a wide and tall butte. A score of feet from its spreading base the rock overhung, providing a roofed aperture between jutting walls of stone.

'A good hole-up there,' the Ranger muttered. 'Come on, feller,' he told the sorrel. 'I'll just put you in the clear and if that mess of up-ended desert heads this way I'll dive in with you.'

He led the sorrel to the cave-like shelter and left him in its depths. Then he returned to the

15

cart. If necessary, he could drive the vehicle into the cleft, where the oxen would also be sheltered.

Hatfield first devoted his attention to the dead owlhoots. They were ornery looking specimens, their distorted features lined by dissipation and full rein given to evil passions.

'Typical border scum,' he mused, 'only rather more intelligent looking than the average. Wonder why in blazes did they cash in that poor devil of a driver like they did? Snake-blooded hellions. Never gave him a chance.'

He glanced apprehensively at the darkening sky. The sun shone a deep, weird magenta color through the pall of yellow dust that swirled and eddied above. To the south was a roaring, blasting hell. But where the salt cart stood was an oasis of comparative calm.

The answer for this was obvious. To the east a long spur of Perdida Mountain ran far into the south. To the west, and near, was a line of tremendous buttes that towered high. Between these two natural walls was a wide amphitheatre shut off from the wind and from the blinding clouds of sand. Dust and particles swirled about the cart, but the full force of the blast was shunted away by the battlements of stone that resisted the wind.

But the great amphitheatre was filled with flying yellow shadows and the scream and moan of the wind. The particles of sand stung Hatfield's face and hands like sparks of fire.

His mouth was dry and gritty. His eyes ached. So long as the wind held steady from the east the gorge was tenable, but should it shift slightly and blow more from the south, he would be in the midst of an inferno.

'Got to find out something about this, though,' he muttered. With a heave of his big shoulders he dumped the body of the owlhoots from the cart. Beneath it was a hollowed out place where the salt had been scooped away. Hatfield set out to enlarge and deepen the hole.

'The hellions weren't digging into that stuff just for fun,' he told himself.

He had hardly begun removing the loose salt when his fingers struck something hard. He realized that the heaped salt that apparently filled the cart was really a layer only a few inches in depth. His groping hands got hold of a rough, irregular fragment of stone. He levered it out and for a moment forgot the storm and its sinister threat.

The stone was seamed and cracked and crumbly, and sprinkled through it, thick as raisins in a pudding, were irregular lumps of a dull yellow color. Also there were crooked 'wires' criss-crossing the surface of the rock. And the fragment was astonishingly heavy for its size.

Hatfield's lips pursed in a soundless whistle. 'Quartz,' he muttered, staring at the fragment, 'broken, crumbly quartz! High-grade gold ore, with about the heaviest metal content I ever laid eyes on. If this darn cart is loaded with the stuff, and I've a notion it is, it's sure worth a mighty big hatful of pesos. No wonder those hellions were after it. Now what in blazes is the answer to this?'

As he stared at the fragment, Goldy suddenly gave a loud snort that was audible even above the roar of the wind. Hatfield's eyes jerked up. With astounding coordination of impulse and muscle he went backward off the cart, turned a complete somersault in the air and landed on his feet back of the vehicle. And at that instant something yelled through the space his body had occupied a split second before. Hands streaking to his guns, he crouched behind the cart and peered into the roaring south.

From the blinding sand cloud had emerged nearly a dozen horsemen. Smoke spurted from the muzzles of their leveled rifles. Bullets spatted the sand, thudded into the sides of the cart, whined between the spokes and under the bed. The Lone Wolf was suddenly on a very hot spot indeed.

Guns out and ready, Hatfield crouched behind the dubious shelter of the spoked wheels. He swore under his breath as lead continued to screech past. The owlhoots had pulled up just clear of the thicker sand cloud and were firing methodically with their rifles. And the distance was too great for his sixes to

18

be effective. His own rifle was in the saddle boot, and for all the good it was likely to do him might as well have been up in the Texas Panhandle.

'Of all the dumb, loco things to do,' Hatfield told himself wrathfully. 'I might have known those hellions were liable to come snukin' back, once they got over their scare and realized I didn't have a posse at my back. Should have kept my saddle gun handy. Well, I'm liable to pay for the mistake with a punctured hide.'

He glanced longingly at Goldy who was watching proceedings with interested eyes. To attempt to cover the near hundred yards to the overhang would be just a nice convenient way to commit suicide. He knew the horse would come to him if he whistled him, but the owlhoots would instantly divine the strategem and would down the sorrel long before he could reach the cart.

A moment before, Hatfield had dreaded a sudden shift of the wind. Now he earnestly desired it. Under cover of the dust he could get in the clear. But the blast continued to howl steadily from east to west. The thick curtain of the sand cloud was clearly defined just beyond the sheltering wall of buttes, and in its shallow fringe, the owlhoots sat their horses and fired with concentrated aim.

A bullet tore a jagged hole in Hatfield's shirt sleeve. Another burned a crease along the side of his neck. A third just flicked his cheek with lethal fingers. The high-wheeled cart afforded but a dubious shelter. Sooner or later one of the slugs was bound to find its mark.

Eyes bleak, face set in grim lines, the Lone Wolf half turned, his muscles tensing. There wasn't a chance in a thousand of his making it, but nevertheless he decided to try a dash for his rifle. Anything was better than being mowed down like a settin' quail.

But even as he turned, from the shadowy depths behind him sounded the clear metallic clang of a rifle. Hatfield sprawled forward on his face.

CHAPTER TWO

Without sound or motion, the Lone Wolf lay. Only his eyes shifted sideways toward the ominous depths of the gorge.

'Surrounded,' he muttered. 'One of the hellions must have snuk around through the dust and got behind me. Well, reckon it's curtains this time.'

The thought flashed through his mind while the echoes of the rifle shot were still banging back and forth among the buttes. Again the heavy boom tore through the dust laden air. Hatfield instinctively ducked closer to the sand. Almost instantly he realized he had heard no whine of passing bullet. Instead, from the dust cloud to the south came loud yells. Screwing his head around he saw one of the owlhoots swaying in his saddle and clutching the horn for support. A third booming report, a wild ducking of heads, and the owlhoots whirled their horses and vanished into a sand storm. A fourth rifle shot speeded them on their way.

Hatfield did not hesitate. He bounded to his feet and streaked for Goldy and his Winchester. He breathed a quick gasp of relief as his hand closed on the walnut stock of the long gun. He jerked it from the boot and whirled about at the sound of clicking hoofs. Rifle at the ready, he waited.

Through the dusty shadows loomed a single rider. Hatfield stood tense. Then his eyes widened with astonishment as a clear, musical voice called—

'Looked like you were on a rather bad spot, cowboy, so I thought I'd better take a hand.'

Hatfield stared. The rider, mounted on a fine roan horse, was a slender, big-eyed girl!

Hatfield found his voice. 'Ma'am,' he said, 'that's putting it sort of mild. I figured I was all set to take the Big Jump. Reckon I would have, if you hadn't happened along just when you did. That was a bad bunch.'

The girl glanced around apprehensively.

'Don't you think we'd better be moving away from here before they get over their scare and decide to come back?' she suggested.

Hatfield chuckled. 'I've a notion they'll keep

on going this time,' he said. 'The storm 'pears to be letting up down there. They're pretty salty, but I don't figure they'll try it again after two bad starts.'

'How did you come to get mixed up with them?' the girl asked.

Hatfield told her, in terse sentences. Her blue eyes darkened and she shook her curly brown head.

'It was a foolhardy thing to do—ride up to a bunch like that all by yourself,' she remarked disapprovingly.

'Reckon mebbe it was,' Hatfield admitted, 'but sometimes a move like that is the best. For all they knew there was a bunch with me, riding hard on my tail. Chances are that's just what they thought. So they trailed their ropes in a hurry. Where I made a mistake was in not figuring they were liable to come back after they got over their first scare and realized I wasn't pounding after them. Then, chances are, they figured it out that I was by myself. Besides, it 'pears they had a good reason for wanting to come back for a look-see.'

'And perhaps the storm was so bad down there they couldn't get through it,' the girl hazarded.

'That's possible, too,' Hatfield agreed. 'Anyhow, they came back, and were making things uncomfortably warm for me.

'Ma'am,' he added, 'you got any notion who they might be?'

22

'I believe,' the girl replied, 'it was Quantrell and his bunch.'

'Who's Quantrell?'

'Nobody knows for sure,' she said. 'To most folks in the section he's just a name—a name that's tied up with everything off-color that's happened here in recent months, and there's been plenty. But he's a killer without an ounce of mercy in his make-up, one of the craftiest rustlers ever heard of and a daring robber. Three times he's held up the stage that runs from the railroad to Gavilan, the cow-town at the head of Espejo Valley. He robbed the Harqua Mine of its clean-up last month.'

'How do folks know Quantrell is responsible for all that hell raising?'

'They don't know,' the girl admitted, 'but all the chores pulled off wear the same brand of efficiency and careful planning. It's hardly reasonable to believe that more than one such outfit is operating in a section, is it?'

'Would look sort of that way, but you never can tell,' Hatfield replied. 'Well, that darn storm is thickening up again. I've a notion we'd better get out of this suck-hole before the wind shifts. By the way, how did you get here, by way of the trail?'

'No,' the girl replied. 'I came down Espejo Valley. There's a track over beside the buttes that turns west from them a few miles north of here and enters the valley mouth. I was riding down this way on the chance of meeting my cousin, Grant Emory. He and the boys are down here somewhere. Yesterday they rode on the trail of a bunch that widelooped a herd from the Forked S ranch and headed for the River. I live at the Lazy R. My name's Sharon Remington.'

Hatfield supplied his own name. The girl reached down a slender, sun-golden little hand and they shook gravely.

'Suppose you ride up to the ranchhouse with me?' she invited. 'It's only a few miles. I've a notion you could use something decent to eat.'

'Notion I could,' Hatfield agreed. 'Figure I'll take you up on that, Ma'am. First, though, I want to look over that poor devil of a driver.'

The girl nodded, and moved back a few paces. Hatfield strode to the slain driver and turned him over on his back. To his surprise the man was not a Mexican *peon* of the sort that usually transported salt from the lakes to the Rio Grande. He was a hard-bitten specimen who showed no signs of Indian blood. He had a straight gash of a mouth across his deeply tanned face, low cheek bones, pale eyes, now set in death, and a shock of hair of a peculiar dead black color that seemed to interest the Ranger.

'Texan, and a miner, judging from the callouses on his hands,' Hatfield mused. He noted the lighter coloring of the man's sunken cheeks.

'Used to wear whiskers, and they grew up

24

almost to his eyes. Scrawny specimen, but looks wiry. Packs a gun like he knew how to use it. No salt freighter, that's for certain, although he might be able to pass for one, especially with that hat pulled down low, if nobody happened to look too close. Chances are that's why he shaved the whiskers off. *Peons* don't often have much beard.'

The driver's pockets discovered nothing of significance. Hatfield was about to turn away when he noticed the corner of what looked to be a sheet of paper protruding from the front of his ragged shirt. He drew it forth. It was paper of a sort having the appearance of ancient sheep-skin manuscript. It was stained with the slain man's blood. Across its surface were drawn fine lines. Hatfield studied it, his black brows drawing together.

'What is it?' the girl asked curiously.

'Looks to be a map,' the Ranger replied. 'A mighty fine piece of work, too.'

'A map of what?'

'Hard to say,' Hatfield replied. 'Look it over. You know this section. Perhaps you can figure something from it.'

The girl took the blood smeared paper gingerly and bent her brows over it in the dim light.

'It is certainly a map of Espejo Valley,' she said. 'I recognize a number of things. Over here to the right is Perdida Peak, with the Dead Star Trail. And see—way up to the right and farther

25

over, the salt flats. And way down to the left is Mule Ears Peak. It's marked plainly—a double peak that looks like a mule's ears. We can see it after we round the buttes. And the western range runs north and curves a little to the east, just as the Perdida Range runs north, only it drops away sharply to the east to widen the valley. But I can't make anything of these lines that criss-cross the thing. I'm sure it's a map of the valley, though.'

Hatfield nodded. He had already arrived at that conclusion.

'The mountain ranges are plainly marked,' he said. 'But the lines drawn seem to run every which way without making any sense. There's a key to it somewhere, of course, but unless you hit on that, the whole thing is meaningless. Just the same, though, I figure I'll hang on to it. Might have something to do with why that poor jigger was cashed in. That and what's in the cart.'

'What's that?'

Hatfield retrieved the fragment of gold ore he had let fall when he dived from the top of the salt cart. The girl eyed it curiously.

'I don't know anything much about such things,' she admitted. 'Perhaps my cousin could tell you where it came from. He is familiar with the mines in this section.'

Hatfield nodded again, and stowed the fragment of rock away. 'I'll hang onto this, too,' he said. He studied the body of the driver.

26

'Reckon we'd better leave him where he is,' he decided. 'Gavilan is the county seat, isn't it? Should be a sheriff there and he'd oughta be notified of what happened down here. Chances are he'd prefer to have the bodies left just where they are. But we'll take the salt cart along with us. Its load is a mite too valuable to leave down here unguarded. You wait here a minute, Ma'am. Keep your rifle ready and an eye on the trail to the south, though I don't think there's anything to worry about.'

He forked Goldy and rode back to the cave that had provided him shelter from the storm. He retrieved his blanket and other belongings. Returning to the cart, he carefully covered the driver's body with the blanket, weighting it down with heavy stones. Those of the two owlhoots he left where they lay.

There was no difficulty in getting the docile oxen turned and lumbering north through the gorge, drawing the creaking cart after them.

'I thought it was funny, when I first saw it, that the feller would be using four head of stock to pull his cart,' Hatfield told Sharon Remington. 'Two is the usual number, and all that's needed. With water scarce like it is on this trail, the drivers don't take along unnecessary animals. What he was pulling is a lot heavier than a cart load of salt.'

As they progressed, the line of buttes, almost a solid wall of stone, veered slightly to the west, with a swelling ridge on the right. A mile or so

27

and the last flanking mass was passed and the glory and splendor of Espejo Valley opened before them.

To the west were mountains, blue and purple against the morning sky, their crests touched with flame. They were little more than five miles distant here in the narrow gut that led to the desert, but fell away sharply as the curve of the valley widened, until in the northwest they were shadowy with distance. To the east were more mountains, much closer, with the towering bulk of Perdida forming their southmost tip. And between the dark walls, a good thirty miles in breadth, was a great grass-grown and wooded cup shimmering like a cluster of emeralds in the sunlight. Far to the northwest was a smudge of smoke against the blue. It marked the site of Gavilan, the cow and mining town at the head of the valley. The mountains on the right veered rather sharply, increasing greatly the width of the valley toward its head, and in the distance Hatfield could just make out the ghostly shimmer of the salt flats that washed their base like a motionless silver sea.

The track they had been following turned more to the west.

'Our ranchhouse is less than two miles from here, over beyond that wooded rise,' the girl said.

'A mighty pretty section,' Hatfield said. 'Looks to be prime cow country. Your cousin owns the spread?'

'No,' Sharon replied. 'I own it. You see Grant Emory is not really my cousin. There is no blood relation between us. My father married again, nearly ten years after my mother died. His second wife was Grant Emory's aunt, and I was taught to call him Cousin Grant. Aunt Liza, as I always called Dad's second wife, died four years ago. Grant worked for a spread up at the head of the valley over next to the salt lakes, and visited us frequently. Then, three months ago, Dad— died. Grant volunteered to come and run the spread for me. He's an excellent cattleman.'

Hatfield nodded. 'Running a big spread is a hefty chore for a girl,' he conceded.

Sharon smiled. 'It's not exactly that,' she explained. 'I'm perfectly capable of running the spread myself. In fact, I did for nearly three years. I was brought up on the range and learned to shoot and ride and rope and brand before I was grown. I was away to school for a couple of years, but when I got back home, Dad was old and none too well. I was, to all practical purposes, his range boss. But you know how cowhands are, I guess. They don't like to work for a woman boss.'

'Loco, but true,' Hatfield admitted.

'So I was glad to have Grant come and take over the chore,' she concluded.

They toiled up the sag, reached its crest, and the Lazy R *casa* and other buildings lay before them in the near distance.

'The spread runs from the desert ten miles north, and from this rise west,' the girl observed.

'West to the mountains?'

'Farther than that,' Sharon replied. 'Our western line is the far slope of that big ridge. Dad obtained title to the Lazy R from the state. Later he included that section of the hills. Why—I don't know. They're nothing but a pile of rocks where nothing will grow. The canyons, and there are lots of them, that cut this side of the ridge, provide shelter from storms and heat, of course, but otherwise the hills have no value so far as anybody has ever known. Dad had some notion about them, though.'

Shortly afterward they drew up to the ranchhouse. Sharon called a wrangler to look after the horses and the oxen. The hand, a grizzled oldtimer, gave Hatfield a sharp look, but asked no questions. Sharon led the way into the house, which was large and well built.

'I'll tell the cook to get busy,' she said, leaving Hatfield in the living room which was spacious and comfortably furnished. Hatfield immediately became interested in the profusion of books in shelves that lined the walls. He was more than a little surprised to note a large number of highly technical works dealing with such subjects as Geology, Petrology, Practical Mining, Advanced Mining Methods, Prospecting as a Science, etc. Jim

Hatfield, graduate of a famous college of engineering, had never lost interest in the subject.

'Somebody hereabouts is more than just a cattleman or cowhand,' he mused.

Seating himself in a roomy chair, he rolled a cigarette and smoked thoughtfully until Sharon rejoined him. A little later they adjourned to the dining room in answer to the cook's call.

Hatfield enjoyed a really good breakfast. He also enjoyed the blue-eyed girl's conversation. She was thoroughly conversant with range work and ranch problems.

'Our troubles here are the usual Big Bend problems,' she observed. 'Getting our beefs to market, and keeping them out of the hands of the wideloopers. Now that the railroad has come through Dorantes to the north the first one is no longer so pressing, but the second I suppose we will always have with us and be forced to deal with it in the same ways.'

'With a gun and a rope?' Hatfield smilingly replied.

'Yes,' the girl agreed, her eyes darkening, 'but I prefer the methods of law and order. That is what we need more than anything else—efficient law enforcement.'

'What's wrong with the sheriff of the county?' Hatfield asked.

Sharon shrugged her slim shoulders.

'Oh, Tom Reeves is all right,' she said, 'but I fear his ability is limited to plenty of courage, strict honesty and a fast gun hand.'

'Good things, all of 'em,' Hatfield chuckled, 'but none of 'em a substitute for brains.'

'And brains are what we are up against here right now, or I'm a lot mistaken,' the girl replied soberly. 'Brains joined with courage, fast gun hands, and—*dis*-honesty.'

'Bad combination,' Hatfield admitted, his black brows drawing together.

A clatter of hoofs sounded outside. Sharon sprang to her feet.

'Here come Grant and the boys!' she exclaimed. 'Oh, somebody has been hurt!'

She ran lightly to the door, onto the veranda and down the steps. Hatfield followed her, gazing at the troop of horsemen who were dismounting in the ranchhouse yard. He counted ten men in all.

Foremost was a tall, well set-up, broad-shouldered man of about thirty. He had a tight-lipped mouth, clear gray, slightly narrow eyes, a prominent nose and high cheek bones. He was darkly tanned, startlingly so in contrast to his pale eyes and the tawny hair that swept back from his big forehead in a crinkly wave. Hatfield rightly surmised that he was Grant Emory.

All of the riders were thickly powdered with the dust of the desert, and all looked exceedingly weary. One man, Hatfield quickly noted, carried his right arm in a sling. The left shoulder of another was roughly bandaged with what looked to be part of a shirt. The bandage showed blood stains. His face was livid and he swayed in his saddle. Two of his companions helped him to dismount.

CHAPTER THREE

'Uh-huh we caught up with 'em, all right,' Grant Emory replied to Sharon Remington's question. 'Ran into them this morning, down on the desert. Trouble is they saw us first. Were all set for us and gunned us proper. Before we could get straightened out they streaked away in that infernal sand storm and we couldn't catch 'em up. Willoby has a hole in his arm. I'm scairt Lem Nelson is bad hurt—bullet through his shoulder.'

Hatfield had drawn near by this time. The girl introduced him.

'This is my cousin, Grant Emory,' she told the Ranger, 'and these are my hands. I've a notion Mr. Hatfield ran into the same bunch,' she told her cousin.

Grant Emory looked the Lone Wolf up and down with hard, suspicious eyes, but his hand was cordial enough.

'How was that?' he asked.

Hatfield told him, stressing Sharon's part in the affair.

'Good work,' grunted Emory. 'Want to hear

more about it, and about that cart load of gold ore. Right now I've got to hightail to town and get the doctor for Willoby and Nelson. I'm worried about Nelson.'

'Suppose you let me have a look at him,' Hatfield suggested. 'I've had a mite of experience with such things.'

Emory eyed him doubtfully, then shrugged his shoulders. 'Reckon yuh can't do any harm,' he grunted. 'It'll take a long time to get the doctor.'

Hatfield hurried to the barn. From his saddlebags he took a small medicine case. He glanced keenly at Nelson who under his instructions had been placed reclining on a blanket. He charged a hypodermic needle with the utmost care with a hundredth-grain portion of a drug and injected it into the wounded man's arm. During his years as a Ranger, he had acquired a not inconsiderable knowledge of medicine and surgery.

'Heart stimulant—nitroglycerin,' he told Emory. 'Figure his heart needs a mite of help.'

With deft, gentle fingers he cut away the blood soaked bandage, laying bare an ugly looking wound low down in Nelson's shoulder. He probed the area with his fingers.

'No bones busted,' was his verdict, 'but it's a bad one, and he's lost a lot of blood.'

He swiftly cleansed the wound, applied an antiseptic salve. Then he bandaged it with an expertness that caused the watching hands to

34

exclaim.

'Feller, if you ain't a sawbones, yuh'd oughta be,' declared Emory.

'Just the same, you'd better get a regular doctor here to have a look at him,' Hatfield replied. 'There's one at Gavilan?'

'Uh-huh,' answered Emory, 'an old jigger who showed up a couple of months back. Got white whiskers and a shorthorn's disposition, but he sure knows his business. Name of McChesney, I rec'lect.'

Hatfield glanced up quickly as Emory pronounced the doctor's name, but proferred no comment other than a nod.

'Get this feller to bed,' he told Emory. 'Four of you pack him on the blanket, and handle him easy.'

Willoby's wound, a clean hole through the flesh of his upper arm, gave the Ranger no concern. He cleansed it, applied a bandage, readjusted the sling.

'You'll be doing your chores again in a couple of weeks,' he told the cowboy.

'And now,' said Emory, 'I'd like to have a look at what's in that cart.'

Under his orders, shovels were brought and the loose salt tossed from the cart, revealing the clumsy body heaped with the valuable ore.

'It looks like Harqua Mine rock,' said Emory, after carefully examining the fragment. 'Uh-huh, looks a heap like it, but I can't be sure. If it is, somebody is sure doin' a prime fancy job of high-gradin' up there. Wonder how in blazes they got it out and didn't get caught doin' it? They ride herd mighty close on the high-grade up there. This load is worth plenty, too.'

Emory's hands were silent as he spoke, but Hatfield, who missed nothing of what went on around him, noted a sardonic gleam in the eyes of one grizzled oldtimer and a derisive twitching of his thin lips.

Emory turned to Sharon. 'I'll have a bite to eat and then I'll ride to town and get Doc,' he told her.

Hatfield spoke up. 'You look sort of peaked, feller, as naturally you would be after bucking that sand storm,' he said. 'I was figuring on riding to town anyhow to give the sheriff the low-down on what happened this morning, so why not let me take the word to the doctor for you?'

Emory glanced around quickly. 'That would be mighty fine of yuh,' he said in grateful tones. 'I admit I don't feel much like buckin' them forty miles right now.'

To Hatfield's surprise Sharon Remington put in a word. 'I think I'll ride with you, Mr. Hatfield,' she said. 'I wanted to get to town today and I'd rather not take the ride alone.'

'Be a pleasure, Ma'am,' Hatfield assured her. From the corner of his eye he noted a quick hardening of Grant Emory's face, a tightening of his lips.

36

But the ranch foreman only nodded his agreement. 'Yuh'll stay in town over night of course?' he remarked to the girl.

'Yes,' Sharon told him.

'I'll try and ride up in the mornin' and come back with yuh,' Emory promised.

'It isn't necessary, Grant,' the girl replied. 'I know you have plenty to do right now, and with two of the boys laid up we'll be short-handed. I'll be all right. Perhaps,' she added, 'Mr. Hatfield will see fit to ride back with me.'

Emory's lips compressed again, but once more he nodded agreement.

'That'll be fine. Hope he will,' he said. He turned on his heel and entered the ranchhouse. The eyes of the old-timer who had been silently listening held a mocking gleam.

A little later, Hatfield and the girl rode north together. For a mile or two they rode practically in silence.

'I've a notion your cousin didn't take it over kind for you to ride to town with me,' the Ranger remarked suddenly.

Sharon's blue eyes danced. 'Grant is consumed with jealousy if I look twice at any man,' she said. 'Poor dear, he fancies he is in love with me.'

'Fancies?'

Sharon glanced around. The Lone Wolf's face was serious, but his strangely colored eyes were sunny as summer seas. Sharon colored prettily, dropped her gaze, and changed the

37

subject.

'Ahead and to the west is the Forked S, the spread that lost the cows yesterday,' she said. 'John Slater owns it. To the east is the Scab Eight, Weston Hale's spread. Then comes the Tadpole and the Fiddle-Back.'

She continued to chatter on about the valley and its inhabitants. Hatfield listened with little comment. Meanwhile his steady eyes were continually studying the terrain and missing nothing. The hills to the west, craggy, dark, slashed by canyons and gorges, seemed to interest him. Their slopes were practically naked, evidently being too rocky or too devoid of moisture to afford root-hold for large growth, although bristles of thicket were in evidence from time to time. The prairie, green and amethyst, heavily grown with grass and boasting numerous groves, stretched to the beginning of the lower slopes where the transition from fertile ground to arid was surprisingly sudden. From the crests of rises they could catch an occasional glimpse of the gray ribbon of the Dead Star Trail winding wearily northward.

They had covered perhaps three-fourths of the distance to town when Sharon gestured to a large white ranchhouse set on a hill to the left.

'That's the Shanghai M *casa*—Talbot Morrow owns it,' she said. 'Talbot was born here, I understand, but he left the section many years ago. He came back six months ago, shortly after old Arnold Morrow, his father, died. Poor fellow, he's a cripple.'

'A cripple?'

'Yes. His legs are paralyzed. He has to be lifted from his chair, and into his buckboard when he wishes to go somewhere. A fine looking man, too. It's a pity.'

Hatfield nodded agreement. 'Always crippled?' he asked.

'No, I guess not,' Sharon replied. 'He was injured some way a few years ago, I was told. I think he was shot. The bullet injured his spine.'

The sun was low in the west when they reached the sprawling cow town set in the shadow of the western hills. Miles farther to the northeast, where the Perdida Range ended, was the weird desolation of the salt flats, dotted with strange, shifting dunes that gleamed like heaps of jewels in the red rays of the setting sun. And on across the flats, its deep depression at times silted with the wind-blown salt, ran the Dead Star Trail.

'The Harqua and the other mines are on that long slope you can see over to the west,' the girl observed as they rode through the straggling outskirts of the town. Their office is here. Perhaps they can tell you something about that gold ore.'

'Reckon I'll drop in and see them after I talk with the sheriff and the doctor,' Hatfield said. 'A place for you to stay here tonight, Ma'am?'

'Yes,' Sharon replied. 'The Cattleman's Hotel is all right. You can get a room there, too, if you wish. They are seldom filled up, except on payday nights.'

They turned into the crooked main street of the town, which was lined with shops, saloons, dance halls and gambling places boasting much plate glass and deceptive false fronts. Here and there a two-storied 'sky-scraper' loomed in dignified isolation. The Cattleman's Hotel was such a spot.

'Right across the street is the doctor's office,' said Sharon. 'I suppose we should stop there first.'

'Good notion,' Hatfield agreed. He tied Sharon's horse, let Goldy's split reins trail on the ground. Together they entered the office.

The old white-bearded doctor looked up, his eyes narrowed a trifle, but he merely grunted a greeting.

'Okay, I'll ride down there in an hour or so,' he replied to their request. 'Yuh say yuh strapped him up, feller? Reckon he'll do all right for a while, then.'

After they left the doctor's office, Hatfield started to take Sharon across the street to the hotel.

'I'm going to the sheriff's office with you first,' she stated. 'After all, I was there too this morning.'

Hatfield gave her a quick glance, then nodded.

They found the sheriff seated at a table, glowering at some reward notices. He was a small man with craggy features and snapping black eyes. His movements were swift and accurate. But his brow wrinkled querulously as if under great mental strain as Hatfield related the details of the encounter on the Dead Star Trail.

'It was Quantrell and his hellions, all right,' the sheriff declared with conviction. 'Yuh say they glommed a herd off the Slash K, too, Miss Remington? Why weren't I notified.'

'I guess the boys didn't want to take the time,' Sharon replied. 'Or perhaps they didn't think of it.'

'Takin' the law in their own hands!' the sheriff growled. 'They'll get in trouble that way some time. All right, I'll ride down to the desert first thing in the mornin'.'

'And now I suppose you'll want to visit the Harqua Mine offices?' Sharon remarked to Hatfield when they were in the street once more.

'Reckon so,' the Ranger agreed. 'I'm taking up a lot of your time, Ma'am.'

'Oh, I'm enjoying it,' Sharon dimpled a reply. 'I thought the sheriff was going to bite me when I told him the boys forgot to tell him about the widelooping. Sheriff Tom takes himself seriously, but I'm afraid nobody else does.'

The Harqua Mine superintendent examined the fragment of ore with great care.

'It looks like some of the rock we have taken from highgrade pockets,' he said finally, 'but I can't be sure without comparing it carefully with specimens known to come from the Harqua. Not that there is much doubt about it in my mind,' he added quickly. 'There is no other ore like this produced any place else in the section. I'm just making the point that the mine cannot claim that cart load on the mere assumption it is from our mine. We would have to definitely establish ownership, a thing difficult to do under the circumstances. Neither of you recognized the driver? No? That's a pity. What I'm much more interested in than the load of ore is how in blazes did they get away from the mine without being detected? We keep a strict watch on our high-grade. Of that you can rest assured.'

'Looks sort of like an inside job,' Hatfield suggested.

'It certainly does,' the super agreed, his face hardening. 'And it will be my urgent business to find out how it was done. I'll hang onto this specimen of ore, if you don't mind, and have it carefully analyzed.'

As they left the mine office, a buckboard drew up before the building and stopped. The driver was a cow-hand. Beside him sat a man with a blanket spread across his knees. He was a handsome man with features of cameo-like regularity, well open, steady blue eyes, and black hair with a touch of gray at the temples. He was erect in bearing, broad of shoulder, deep of chest, and evidently of good height. His hands, that lay motionless on his blanketed knees, Hatfield noticed, were broad, muscular and deeply bronzed.

Sharon nodded to him, and the man nodded back without speaking.

'It's Talbot Morrow,' the girl said in low tones as they passed on.

'Nice looking jigger,' Hatfield commented.

'Yes, he is,' Sharon agreed, 'and he seems to be very nice, too, although he has very little to say. Men who work for him say he knows the cattle business. He keeps his ranch in fine shape and raises first class beef. I think he has an interest in the Harqua Mine also. He often stops to chat with the superintendent.'

At the hotel Hatfield established Sharon in a comfortable room. He also secured one for himself.

'I'm going out to do some shopping,' the girl told him. 'See you in the morning.'

'Okay,' Hatfield agreed. 'I'll look after the horses. There's a livery stable on the alley around the corner, I understand.'

Before attending to the chore, however, Hatfield paused in his room. He lighted the lamp that stood on a table, took the blood

43

smeared map of Espejo Valley from his pocket and spread it under the light. As he bent over it, his brows suddenly drew together. In the strong light he saw what he had missed in the gloom of the gorge.

Almost obliterated by the blood smear were tiny letters. With some difficulty he spelled them out—

V of Perdida to Harqua—Perdida W

'Now what in blazes?' he wondered. 'Doesn't seem to make any sense.'

He examined the writing again, shaking his black head over it.

'That's sure what it 'pears to make out,' he growled—"*V of Perdida to Harqua—Perdida W.*" Must have some meaning, but what? I've a notion it means plenty, all right.'

He studied the lines drawn on the paper and came to the conclusion that Sharon Remington had been right in her guess. It was undoubtedly a map of the valley. The hills to the west, the wide upper portion, the narrow neck that led to the desert, with Perdida Peak shown with exaggerated prominence at the southern tip of the Perdida Range. The position of the Harqua Mine, he decided, was designated by a tiny circle on the slope west of the town.

'Looks like maybe it points out the route that should be followed by whoever lifts the

44

highgrade from the mine,' he mused. 'But the lettering has sure got me guessing. No, it doesn't seem to make sense, but I'll bet a hatful of pesos it's the key to the whole thing.'

Finally, with a baffled exclamation, he folded the sheet compactly and stowed it with the note in the secret pocket of his belt.

The livery stable proved satisfactory. Hatfield secured accommodations for Goldy and Sharon's roan. Then he sauntered along the main street with a big steak in mind.

A large saloon that boasted a long lunch counter and tables for more leisurely patrons caught his eye. He entered, found a table and gave his order to a white-aproned waiter. He looked the place over with interest.

Although it was barely dusk, the big room was already pretty well crowded. The occupants were chiefly cowhands, drinking at the bar, eating, bucking the roulette wheels, the faro bank, or absorbed in poker. As the darkness deepened, numbers of miners in muddy boots and red or blue woolen shirts trooped in. Local shopkeepers and workers were also in evidence.

What interested Hatfield more was a sprinkling of individuals who wore rangeland garb and looked like cowhands, but who, the Ranger decided, were not.

'Notion this pueblo is a sort of stopping off place for gents on their way from the north to the Border, or the other way around,' he mused. 'Some salty looking members here.'

As he ate he was conscious of more than one sideways glance cast in his direction. Evidently a stranger came in for a careful going-over.

Indeed it struck Hatfield that there was a tenseness about the place, a furtive air of suspicion held in leash but nevertheless apparent. As if nobody was quite sure about his neighbor.

'Reckon no gent is certain but what the jigger standing next to him may be Quantrell or one of his outfit,' the Ranger decided.

After finishing his meal, Hatfield sat for some time smoking, apparently deep in thought. Finally he pinched out his cigarette butt and rose to his feet.

'Figure I'll show this loco map to the mine superintendent and see if he can make anything of it,' he told himself. 'Recall he said he was going to work late tonight and might find time to give that hunk of rock a going over.'

Shortly after leaving the saloon he turned up a quieter side street on which the mine office building was located some little distance from the main thoroughfare. He was pleased to note a dim glow shining back of the dusty window panes. With light, almost noiseless steps he entered the building through the open main door, followed a deserted corridor for a short distance and reached the door of the super's

46

office. He raised his hand to knock, then saw that the door stood nearly half open. He stepped forward, his glance seeking the official's desk. Then with bewildering speed he hurled himself sideways and down. A gun boomed, a slug hissed past his face and thudded into the wall.

Hatfield jerked his guns as a shadowy figure leaped forward and swept the lighted lamp from the super's desk. Darkness blanketed the room as through it gushed lances of reddish fire. The walls rocked to the roar of six shooters.

Twisting, writhing on the floor, changing position each time he pulled trigger, Hatfield answered the blazing guns shot for shot. Bullets slashed the floor around him, knocked splinters into his face, thudded into the wall. He felt one rip his sleeve, another whip his hat sideways on his head. There was a clatter of breaking glass and splintering wood. Hatfield bounded to his feet and leaped forward, guns ready. He collided with a body, slashed out with a gun barrel. He heard the man grunt with pain. Then fingers like rods of nickel steel bit into his shoulders. He was hurled sideways with prodigious force. He staggered, reeled, pitched over an unseen chair and hit the floor with a crash. Before he could regain his feet there was a second clattering of glass followed by a patter of swift feet outside the smashed window.

47

CHAPTER FOUR

For tense moments Hatfield lay where he had fallen, listening intently. The room was very still save for a mumbling mutter over to one side. Finally he got cautiously to his feet once more, listened, took a chance and fumbled a match. He struck it, held it at arm's length an instant and dashed it to the floor. The quick flare had shown him he was alone in the room save for a huddled form against the far wall that moved feebly.

Hatfield risked another match. He shot a quick glance at the form on the floor. Its movements were more vigorous, but still uncoordinated.

The desk lamp was smashed, but there was a bracket lamp on the wall nearby. Hatfield touched the match flame to the wick. A moment later the room was bathed in a soft glow. He strode across to the prostrate man and turned him over on his back. He uttered an exclamation as he recognized the superintendent.

The super opened his eyes, stared blankly at the Ranger bending over him. Another moment and he fully regained consciousness. Hatfield propped him into a sitting position.

'What happened?' he asked.

'Dunno,' mumbled the super. 'I was working at my desk and turned around when I heard a sound behind me. Got a glimpse of two men wearing black masks. Then one hit me over the head with something—a gun barrel, I reckon. Don't remember anything else.'

Hatfield helped him to his feet, guided him to a chair.

'Got a knot on your head, but figure it's nothing serious,' he decided after a swift examination. 'But they sure made a mess of your office.'

Which was decidedly not an overstatement. Drawers had been jerked out, their contents dumped and scattered about. A filing case had been emptied on the floor. Papers from the desk were scattered on the floor.

Outside was a sound of shouting, drawing swiftly nearer. A moment more and boots pounded in the corridor. Several men rushed into the office. In the lead was Sheriff Tom Reeves. He glared suspiciously at Hatfield.

'What the hell's goin' on here?' he demanded harshly.

Hatfield and the super told him, briefly. The sheriff swore.

'What in blazes were they after?' he asked.

'That's what I'd like to know,' grunted the super. 'There's nothing of value ever kept here. We don't even have a safe.'

'Well, they sure gave the place a goin' over,' growled the sheriff. He turned to Hatfield.

'You get a look at 'em?'

'Not much,' the Ranger replied. 'About all I really saw was the blaze of a gun before the light went out. They sure threw lead fast for a minute and then went through the window.'

'Big fellers?' asked the sheriff.

'Reckon one was pretty sizeable, from the way he took hold of me,' Hatfield replied. 'Had a grip like a bear trap.'

'Figger yuh hit either one of 'em?'

'I figger I hit one, with a gun barrel, from the way he yelped when I swiped at him. Don't reckon any of my lead connected. No blood spots anywhere.'

The sheriff swore some more.

'Well,' he declared, 'they'd sure oughta got some scratches goin' through the glass. That's somethin' to be keepin' a eye open for—gents with chopped up faces. Not that the hellions wouldn't have a alibi for it. I figger they got plenty of savvy. Come on, you fellers,' he told his companions. 'We'll look the ground over outside and see if we can pick up a trail. Reckon they scooted down the alley. You all right, Hodges?' he asked the super.

'Oh, I'm okay, aside from a headache,' the mine official replied. 'I'll start straightening up this mess.'

'I'll lend you a hand,' Hatfield offered.

The sheriff hesitated, shooting a swift glance at the Lone Wolf, but when the super accepted the offer the sheriff made no comment. A

50

moment later his boots pounded down the corridor.

'It sure beats me,' said the super, as they began replacing drawers and righting chairs. 'I can't imagine what they were after. I was just going to give that ore fragment a going over with a microscope when—say, where is that chunk, anyhow? It was right here on my desk.'

A thorough search of the room failed to discover the fragment.

'Reckon one of the hellions pocketed it,' the super finally decided. 'Well, it doesn't matter. They can send up another chunk from the cart. They got it down at the Lazy R, I believe you said.'

Hatfield nodded, his eyes thoughtful. After the office was straightened up somewhat he broached the subject of his visit.

The super took the map and studied it. 'It's a map of the valley,' he agreed, 'but that seems to be all. Let's go over it with a glass and see if we can find anything more.'

But a careful scrutiny of the paper revealed nothing more, the glass merely corroborating Hatfield's translation of the minute letters beneath the blood stain.

'And what that means is anybody's guess,' said the super. 'I've a notion your supposition is right—it plots the route to be taken by the highgraders. Only it doesn't show where they go after leaving the valley—Mexico, I suppose. Easy to dispose of the ore down there.'

51

Hatfield nodded, but said nothing. The concentration furrow was deep between his black brows. A sure sign the Lone Wolf was doing some hard thinking.

'Well,' said the super, 'things are in pretty good shape again. I think I'll go home. My head doesn't feel so good.'

They left the office together. At the Cattleman's Hotel, where the official had a room, Hatfield said goodnight. He walked slowly along the main street, still thinking deeply. He had just reached the swinging doors of the Ace Full saloon when a man came out. It was Grant Emory. His face was scratched and bruised and he looked to be in a very bad temper. He recognized Hatfield and grunted a greeting.

'I don't know what this section is comin' to,' he barked indignantly. 'Gettin' so a man ain't safe anywhere. I was just ridin' into town when a coupla hellions came skalleyhootin' along the trail hell-bent for election. They barged smack into me, knocked my horse plumb off his feet and stood me on my head in the dirt. Before I could get myself together and unlimber my gun they were out of sight in the brush. Sure wish I could have lined sights with the sidewinders. I feel all stove up.'

'Get a look at them?' Hatfield asked.

'Hell, no,' growled Emory. 'There waren't much light and they were a-streakin' it. All I saw was a coupla big jiggers loomin' up in front of me when their horses, or one of 'em, hit mine. I was just moseyin' along, so they had the advantage. Where's Sharon?'

'In her room at the hotel by now, I reckon,' Hatfield replied. 'She had some shopping chores to do, but the chances are she finished 'em by this time.'

'Okay, let's go back in and have a drink together, then,' said Emory. 'I'll ride back to the spread with her tomorrow. By the way, are yuh hangin' around in this section or just passin' through?'

'Haven't made any connections yet,' Hatfield evaded. 'Might hang around if I can tie onto a job of riding.'

Emory looked speculative. 'Gettin' close to roundup time,' he observed. 'Easy for a tophand to tie up with an outfit. Keep your cinch tight until tomorrow. I want to speak to Sharon, then I'd like to have a talk with yuh.'

'Okay,' Hatfield agreed. 'Let's get that drink.'

As they stood at the bar discussing their drink and talking, the swinging doors pushed open and a man entered, a slim, immaculate looking man who lent an air of elegance to his homely range attire. He had a thin, strongly featured face, a crisp mustache and an aggressive tuft of beard on his prominent chin. His eyes, Hatfield noted, were a cold light blue, the blue of a glacier lake. He glanced swiftly about, his gaze fixed on Emory and his finely

53

formed lips twisted in a derisive smile.

Hatfield saw Emory flush, his jaw tighten, his hands ball into fists. He met the other's gaze, his own eyes hard and defiant. But no word was spoken. The newcomer passed to the far end of the bar, walking with easy grace, his shoulders square, his slender body erect with soldierly bearing.

'Bad blood between those two,' Hatfield told himself, with conviction. He wondered who the man might be. Grant Emory supplied the deficiency.

'Walsh Knox, Talbot Morrow's foreman,' he remarked, jerking his head at the receding back of the other. 'Morrow owns the Shanghai M, one of the best spreads in the section. He's a cripple.'

'I saw him today, sitting in his buckboard in front of the Harqua Mine office,' Hatfield said.

Emory nodded. 'Uh-huh, he's in bad shape. Knox runs the spread for him. A salty jigger, Knox.'

'Looks it,' Hatfield agreed.

Before Emory could make any further remark, the doors swung open and Sheriff Reeves entered looking very much disgruntled. His gaze fixed on Emory's scratched face and Hatfield saw his eyes narrow. He walked up to the foreman.

'What happened to you?' he demanded.

Emory repeated the story he told Hatfield. The sheriff listened, his face expressionless.

For a moment he was silent, then he turned to Hatfield.

'Couldn't find hide or hair of the hellions,' he said. 'We combed the whole section. That alley back of the office twists around among the shacks and dobes the miners live in and there are plenty of holes they coulda slid into.'

'Didn't figure you'd have much luck,' Hatfield remarked.

Emory glanced inquiringly from one to the other. Hatfield explained what happened in the mine office. Emory shook his head, and swore.

'This section is gettin' worse every day,' he growled.

'That's right,' the sheriff agreed grimly. 'Been gettin' worse and worse for the past six months.

The observation sounded innocent enough, but Hatfield saw Emory's jaw tighten. However, he made no comment.

'I'll ride down to the desert as soon as it's light, and have a look at those jiggers,' the sheriff told Hatfield. 'Yuh better stick around in case McChesney wants to hold an inquest. He's coroner.'

'Okay,' Hatfield agreed, 'and while you're at it, Sheriff, stop at The Lazy R and pick up another hunk of that ore from the cart. The mine superintendent wants to make a comparison with the Harqua highgrade. Those hellions tied onto the specimen I brought to town.'

'I'll do it,' said the sheriff. 'Well, be seein' yuh. I'm goin' to drop my loop on a mite of shut-eye.'

'Figure I'll do the same thing,' Hatfield replied. 'Didn't get overmuch last night, and it's been a long day.'

The sheriff nodded and departed. Emory stared after him.

'Yuh say those jiggers went through the window?' he asked slowly.

'And took it with them,' Hatfield answered.

Emory rasped his chin with his forefinger. 'And were purty apt to have gotten a mite scratched up doin' it,' he said. 'I see why Reeves gave me such a once-over. He don't think over well of me anyhow. Well, I did get bunged up by bein' knocked off my horse, no matter what he thinks.'

'He didn't accuse you of anything,' Hatfield pointed out.

'No,' agreed Emory morosely, 'but I know damn well what he was thinkin'. Oh, hell, let's go to bed.'

Hatfield offered no objection to the suggestion and they left the saloon together. At the hotel, Emory said goodnight and passed on to his own room, farther down the corridor. Hatfield entered his room and lighted a lamp. He glanced around, his gaze fixed on the white pillow at the head of his bed, and held.

Pinned to the pillow slip was a fragment of smeary paper. Across it was pencilled a rude

56

scrawl. Hatfield's eyes narrowed as he read the two words—

Git out

The writing was undoubtedly the same as that on the warning note in his secret pocket.

CHAPTER FIVE

Hatfield awoke early the following morning. He was seated by the window, smoking a cigarette and thinking, when a knock sounded at the door. He opened it to admit Grant Emory.

'Me and Sharon were just headin' out for breakfast,' said the foreman. 'She wants yuh to go along.'

'Okay,' Hatfield agreed. 'Be plumb pleased to.'

'I wanted to talk to you,' the girl said after they were seated at a table in the hotel dining room. 'I spoke with Grant about the matter and he agrees with me. We are left shorthanded right now, and with the roundup season coming on. Would you care to sign up with the Lazy R? Grant needs an assistant badly. Some of our boys are pretty old, and most of the others are young and a trifle wild.'

'Good hands, but reg'lar young hellers,'

Emory put in. 'They know their chores, but they need somebody to hold 'em down all the time. I can't be everywhere at once, and with things like there are in this section I'd like mighty well to have a man on hand who can carry out orders and see that others carry 'em out, too. What yuh say, feller?'

Hatfield considered a moment. He had arrived at no definite decision relative to the status of Emory, but one thing he had definitely decided—that the Lazy R was likely to be the focal point, in one way or another, of what went on in the section. A job with the outfit would give him a logical excuse for hanging around.

'Reckon I could do worse,' he obliquely accepted the proferred job.

'Fine!' applauded Emory. Sharon Remington smiled and looked pleased.

'We'll start back for the spread as soon as we finish eating,' she decided.

When they arose from the table, Hatfield excused himself for a short time.

'I'll be with you by the time you're ready to head south,' he told his companions. 'I want to see Hodges, the mine super, a minute.'

He found Hodges in his office, apparently none the worse for his harrowing experience of the night before. He greeted Hatfield cordially.

'Feel okay,' he told the Ranger. 'Head is a little sore, but no aches.'

'Glad to hear it,' Hatfield said. 'By the way, suh, I believe you said the two jiggers who

58

larruped you were masked?'

'That's right,' Hodges agreed. 'I saw that much, anyhow.'

'Handkerchief around the lower part of the face?' Hatfield asked.

'Hodges shook his head. 'No, their faces were completely covered, except for eyeholes. I'd say they had the masks strapped tight around their heads. Not a chance to see their features—only the glint of eyes through the holes.'

Hatfield nodded, apparently pleased at what he had just heard. He thanked the super and departed, promising to have another specimen of the ore sent him for examination.

'Fact is I told Sheriff Reeves to pick up a chunk and bring it along with him on his way back from the desert,' he explained.

A little later Hatfield rode south with Sharon and Grant Emory. They rode steadily at a good pace until they were passing over the Forked S range, just north of the Lazy R holdings. Here Emory pulled up.

'You and Sharon mosey on to the *casa*,' he told Hatfield. 'I'm goin' to slide over to John Slater's place and find out if him and his boys got any line on them wide-loopers. Be seein' yuh a little later.'

He turned west across the prairie. Hatfield and Sharon continued on south. Finally they came in sight of the Lazy R ranchhouse. As they drew near they observed a man pacing backward and forward across the veranda with short, jerky strides.

'It's Sheriff Reeves!' exclaimed Sharon, 'and something is bothering him. He always prances that way when he's put out over something.'

They dismounted in front of the ranchhouse and ascended the steps to join the sheriff who was looking very irritable indeed.

'Are you plumb loco?' he barked at Hatfield.

'Can't say for sure,' the Lone Wolf returned. 'Reckon I'll leave that to other folks' judgment.'

The sheriff glared at him accusingly. 'If yuh leave it to me, I'm of a mind to answer yes,' he declared. 'Thought yuh told me there were three bodies for me to look over down there on the Dead Star Trail at the edge of the desert!'

'Come to think of it, believe I did,' Hatfield returned.

'Well, yuh're either loco or yuh were seein' things!' growled the sheriff. 'There sure ain't none down there now.'

'No?'

'No! And that's just what I mean. We didn't find even one, much less three. Yuh sure yuh didn't make up that yarn yuh told me?'

'Sheriff Tom,' Sharon put in before Hatfield could speak, 'remember I also saw them.'

The sheriff glared at her in turn, an expression of personal injury on his face.

'Well, they ain't there now,' he repeated. 'What in blazes become of them?'

60

'I'd say,' Hatfield supplied, 'that somebody must have taken them away.'

'But in the name of blazes, why?'

'I don't think the problem is a very obscure one,' the Lone Wolf replied. 'I'd say because they didn't want anybody in this section to get a good look at them. Perhaps they were scared somebody would recognize them and tie them up with somebody else.'

The sheriff stared at him, his brows wrinkling querulously but quickly clearing as the notion sank in.

'By gosh, I believe yuh're right!' he exclaimed. He turned to Sharon.

'You didn't recognize either of 'em?'

Sharon slowly shook her head. 'I really didn't look at them,' she replied with a slight shudder. 'They were not a very pretty sight, sprawled out on the sand and covered with blood. When Mr. Hatfield began examining them, I moved away and turned my head.'

'Reckon that's nacherel, but I sure wish yuh hadn't been so squeamish,' the sheriff remarked gloomily. 'Well, wimmen folks are wimmen folks, and there ain't no changin' 'em. Well, reckon I might as well get back to town.'

'I slipped up by not having her look over them,' admitted Hatfield. 'Don't forget to take that specimen of the gold ore back with you.'

'Okay,' grunted the sheriff. 'Get me a hunk.'

Sharon called the old wrangler, who, having cared for the horses, was pottering about

61

nearby.

'Get a specimen of that ore from the car,' she directed. 'Grant had the cart put behind the barn, I believe.'

The old fellow nodded, and bow-legged off. He was back in a few minutes, empty-handed.

'Ma'am, yuh sure Grant put that cart behind the barn?' he asked.

'Why, yes,' Sharon replied. 'I saw it done.'

'Well,' drawled the wrangler, 'them oxes is grazin' in the side pasture, but there ain't no cart behind the barn or nowhere else I can see.'

His auditors stared at him, then with one accord hurried to the barn.

The wrangler wasn't suffering from an attack of loco. The cart was not there, nor anywhere in sight. Sheriff Reeves even looked inside the barn with barren results.

Hatfield studied the short, firm turf with keen eyes.

'It was here, all right,' he said. 'You can see the wheel marks plain where it stood, and farther on, very faint, are the tracks made when it was moved away. Also, there are prints of horses' irons.'

The sheriff said something under his breath that was certainly not fitting for a lady's ears. Aloud he remarked,

'That load must have been almighty valuable, for them to take a chance on snukin' it away from here.'

'Yes,' Hatfield agreed quietly. 'Chances are,

a lot more valuable than we had any notion.'

Sharon glanced at him quickly, but Hatfield did not see fit to elaborate on his rather cryptic remark.

'Well,' said the sheriff, "I'm headin' back to town, before the hellions wideloop the jail. Ain't nothin' safe hereabouts any more. Yes, I'll have somethin' to eat before I go, Sharon, but I can't spend the night. I want to head off Doc McChesney before he starts back down here in the mornin' with his coroner's jury and grave diggers. There ain't nothin' for him to set on, or plant.'

They returned to the ranchhouse. 'You take the little room there off the living room,' Sharon told Hatfield. 'There's no room in the bunkhouse for you right now. Grant sleeps in the room over you, if you should want him for anything.'

After the meal was eaten, Sheriff Reeves said goodbye and headed for town. Hatfield finished a cigarette and rose to his feet.

'I figure to take a little ride, Ma'am,' he told Sharon.

The girl glanced at him questioningly, but only nodded. Hatfield went to get the rig on Goldy. Grant Emory had not yet showed up when he rode away from the ranchhouse and headed south along the route they had taken from the desert's edge the morning before. Shortly after he was out of sight from the ranchhouse, he veered to the east. Soon he reached the Dead Star Trail that curved, lonely and deserted, around the vast bulk of Perdida Peak.

*   *   *

Jim Hatfield had heard the legend of the old and mysterious trail, once trod by Coronado and the iron men of Spain, and immeasurably ancient when the Spaniard first set mailed foot on the soil of Texas. The name, 'The Dead Star Trail' came from the people of the Aztec, but not of the Aztecs. It was born, it was said, in the mouths of the strange and mystic folks who were there before the Aztec arrived in the land. From them came the weird legend of the making of the trail.

In the beginning, it was said, all the stars were holy. Humble in their beauty, shining with a light white and clear. But in the breast of one star grew pride, and from pride came evil. The clear, white light of the evil star changed to a sullen and baleful red that affrighted the white and holy stars. But the Thunder Bird, Spirit of Good, rose in wrath from his perch on the rim of the sun. His mighty wings, beneath which the earth could cower as a nestling, spread wide. Across the unmeasured reaches of space he sped and plunged his beak into the heart of the evil star and slew it, so that it fell, burned and blackened, through countless ages until it reached the earth. Southward it rolled, down

64

the long slopes, past the lonely mountains, across the fiery desert and plunged into the canyoned waters of the Rio Grande and was lost forever. But behind it trailed the mark of its passing, crooked and burned and blackened, down the long slopes, in the shadow of the lonely mountains and across the fiery desert, even to the waters of the Rio Grande. The old and mystic people named the fearful track The Dead Star Trail, and called it a road by which evil would travel. And throughout the ages The Dead Star Trail did not belie its name.

South and southwest of Perdida Mountain, southern battlement of the Perdida Range, stretches the desert, an arid waste of sand and salt and alkali. Grotesque buttes and chimney rocks start up from its burning floor, and strange, symmetrical spires that almost seem to be monuments set by the hand of man, instead of what they are—tombstones to ages long dead. Farther west are mountains, a purple shadow against the Texas sky, and farther to the south, beyond the Rio Grande, are other mountains, darkly blue, crowned with white, the mountains of Mexico.

To the west and north of Perdida is rangeland, rich in grass and curly mesquite. The old Spaniards mined much gold and silver from Perdida's stony breast, legend says, but no modern prospector ever found traces of precious metal in the Perdida Range. On the northern slopes of the mountains that form the western wall of wide Espejo Valley are mines of value, their dark tunnel mouths gaping down at the cattle and mining town of Gavilan; the most valuable of them is the big Harqua Mine where rich pockets of high-grade ore are found.

*   *   *

Now Hatfield rode slowly, scanning the surface of the trail. Soon his search was rewarded. Plainly indenting the soft surface were the twin wheel marks of the salt cart.

'Figured they'd head this way,' he muttered exultantly. 'Now to run the hellions down.'

Until the trail veered southwest across the desert the wheel marks continued on its surface. But not far below the cave in which Hatfield spent the night they turned to the east, following a dim track that hugged the slope of the spur that ran southward from the main body of the mountain.

Mile after mile Hatfield rode. To the west and south was the desert, but a belt of more fertile soil, thickly grown with tall brush, flanked the slope and extended some distance toward the sand. At times the track ran between walls of brush that was higher than the head of a mounted man.

Hatfield rode carefully, eyeing the trail ahead with keen eyes, listening for any significant sound. The nature of the tracks told him that he was travelling considerably faster than the clumsy cart had done.

66

'They must have holed it up somewhere or emptied it and packed the stuff off,' he told himself. 'Either way, there's a chance to get a line on where they're heading.'

Another mile was covered, with the brush crowding thickly on either side of the trail. Large patches of grass and occasional bushes growing tall on the track proved that it was little used, although there was evidence that it might have been considerably travelled years before. Hatfield became even more watchful. It was doubtful if the heavily loaded vehicle had been dragged for any great distance, and he was already nearly twenty miles from the ranchhouse.

Suddenly his head jerked to the right. Somewhere in the brush there had sounded a sharp thud. His hands dropped to his guns, and at the same instant a voice rang out on his left—

'Hold it! Yuh're covered!' The sharp click of a gun hammer drawn back to full cock emphasized the command.

CHAPTER SIX

Hatfield 'held it.' There was nothing else to do. He was 'caught settin'.'

'All right,' ordered the unseen speaker. 'Raise your hands—slow, and empty. Up high.

67

And keep 'em there.'

As Hatfield obeyed, there was a crackling on the brush to his left. An instant later three masked men stepped into view, cocked guns menacing the Ranger. Two were squat, powerful looking individuals. The third, who did the talking, was taller and of more slender build.

'Don't worry about what's over there to the right,' he said in a jeering voice. 'That was just a rock I chucked over there to make yuh look around. Yuh fell for it, all right, just as yuh fell for the cart trick. Looks like old McDowell's extra smart jigger ain't so smart after all—to fall for a trick like that. Figgered yuh wouldn't be able to keep from tryin' to trail the cart, so we just holed up and waited for yuh to come along. Was told to keep outa this section, wasn't yuh? Well, yuh wouldn't listen. Yuh played a purty dangerous game, and it looks like yuh lost it. Now us fellers will call showdown—and yuh didn't fill your hand!'

Hatfield said nothing, although he was inwardly seething with rage, more at himself than against the speaker. He had walked into the trap with his eyes wide open. And he knew he had a mighty good chance of paying dearly for his mistake. Meanwhile, he was staring with interest at the mask that covered the speaker's face. The lower part of it, where it covered the chin, jutted out in a peculiar fashion.

'Get his hardware, Gulden,' the tall man

directed. 'Get that saddle gun, too. Careful, now, he's tricky, and lightnin' fast. Don't take no chances. Watch out for that horse, too. I've a notion he's plumb bad.'

One of the squat men approached Hatfield from the rear, reached up gingerly and unbuckled his cartridge belts. He withdrew the Winchester from the saddle boot, and stepped back.

'Okay,' said the leader. 'Parks, go fetch the horses.'

The second squat man pushed his way into the brush to reappear a few minutes later leading three saddled and bridled horses. At the leader's direction, he and Gulden mounted. They trained their guns on Hatfield while the leader forked his own cayuse.

'Now ride right ahead,' he told Hatfield. 'Take it easy, and don't try no tricks. That yaller horse looks fast, but a slug of lead is a heap sight faster. Yuh can put your hands down now.'

With Hatfield riding a few paces in front of his captors they got under way. For some two miles they followed the track that now wound almost due east around the southern tip of the spur. Suddenly, however, just after rounding a bend, the tall leader called a halt. Gulden rode forward, turned his horse directly toward the wall of growth that flanked the trail on the left. The growth extended up the slope of the spur in an apparently solid bristle.

Gulden rode straight for the fringe of chaparral, forced his horse into it, and vanished.

'All right,' the leader called to Hatfield. 'Foller Gull, and don't forget we're in front and behind yuh.'

Hatfield obeyed orders. Goldy snorted protest at entering the apparently solid wall of brush, but obeyed Hatfield's word of command. A crackling and swaying and he was through what was really but a thin straggle of growth, although a man riding within a yard of it would not have noticed the fact. Ahead stretched a narrow lane cut through the chaparral for a distance of perhaps twenty yards, ending in a dark opening in the swelling rise of the slope.

At the mouth of the opening Gulden was waiting. Hatfield rode on, the irons of the other two clicking on the stones behind him. He pulled to a halt at Gulden's grunted order. Gulden dismounted and vanished into the opening, leading his horse. A few minutes later a light flared in the darkness. Gulden reappeared, holding aloft a lighted lantern.

'Unfork, and go on in,' the leader told Hatfield.

Hatfield obeyed, following Gulden and his bobbing lantern along a low, fairly wide passage. A quick glance or two decided him that the corridor was an old mine tunnel. Behind him he could hear his other two captors scuffing along in his wake, the irons of their led horses ringing on the rock floor.

For perhaps fifty yards the tunnel burrowed into the mountain. Then abruptly it widened into a room hewn in the stone, a room some thirty feet in width. Ahead, about the same distance, he could make out the continuance of the narrower tunnel.

'Hold it,' growled Gulden. He placed the lantern on a rough board table, struck a match and proceeded to light several lamps bracketed into the stone walls. Hatfield gazed about with interest at the owlhoots' hideout.

The room had been roughly fitted up as a living quarters. Several bunks were built along the walls. There were some home-made chairs, a dutch oven, a number of cooking utensils, some coarse crockery, and a supply of staple provisions on a shelf. Over to one side was a hitchrack capable of accommodating a dozen horses. To this rack the owlhoots tethered their mounts and Goldy. Then they turned their attention to Hatfield.

The tall man's gaze was speculative, but Gulden's eyes gleamed hotly through the holes in his mask. He stepped up to the Ranger, muttering under his breath.

'Well, reckon yuh don't feel so peart as yuh did the other mornin' when yuh plugged my bunky!' he growled. Barking an oath, he slapped Hatfield across the face, hard, with his open hand.

Hatfield said nothing. He made no move. He merely looked at Gulden. For a moment the owlhoot met the steady green eyes, then he dropped his own glance, edged back a step, muttering, and slid a hand to his gun butt.

'Hold it!' exclaimed the tall leader. 'Yuh know what the Boss's orders were. Yuh wanta tangle with *him?* Stop that damn foolishment and search this jigger.'

Still muttering, Gulden obeyed, the man Parks assisting.

They did a thorough job, searching him to the skin, forcing him to remove his boots and carefully examining them inside. Finally they stepped back with baffled remarks.

'He ain't got it,' growled Gulden.

The tall man eyed Hatfield, mechanically raising his hand to his masked chin.

'Reckon he ain't,' he agreed, 'but he knows where it is, yuh can bet on that. Okay, we'll fasten him up and hold him for the Boss. The Boss has ways of makin' a jigger talk, even if he don't hanker to.'

'I'll make him talk, if yuh give me the chance,' rumbled Gulden. 'I'd sure like to have the chance. I'm in favor of cashin' him in right now—it's the safest thing to do.'

'Mebbe so,' admitted the leader, 'but orders is orders. Okay, herd him back inter the hole and we'll fasten him up.' He stepped to the little heap of Hatfield's belongings on the table beside his holstered guns, picked up his tobacco and matches and thrust them at him.

'Here,' he grunted, 'reckon yuh can stand a smoke while yuh're waitin'. I wouldn't take that away from a feller what ain't got much time, even if he is a blankety-blank Ranger.'

For the first time since his capture, Hatfield spoke.

'Much obliged, feller,' he said. 'Mebbe I'll remember it some time.'

'Reckon not,' the other replied significantly. 'Not after tonight. Never mind your boots. Yuh won't need boots where yuh're goin'.'

They herded the Ranger into the continuance of the tunnel, Gulden bearing the lantern. For some sixty paces the tunnel ran straight, with unbroken walls, then an opening yawned on the left. Into this Hatfield was forced. Gulden held the lantern high, and Hatfield's breath caught in his throat.

The room, about ten yards square, had evidently been used as a storehouse of sorts. Rusty picks and shovels and bars of curious design were scattered about. But there were also other things.

Some six feet out from the far wall was a row of thick iron rods set into the rock floor and the rock ceiling to form uprights about three feet apart. The row continued around the far end wall also, Hatfield noted. To these uprights were secured stout chains riveted to the iron. The chains ended in ponderous leg irons, and nearly all of the iron cuffs were locked about what had once been a human ankle, but now was fleshless bone.

Some lying prone, some hunched over with knees drawn up to the bony chins were the pitiful victims. In most cases the corpses had dried and dessicated in the hot, dry air, until instead of skeletons, they had become grotesque mummies with parchment skin drawn tight over the bones beneath, eyeless sockets staring, shrivelled lips drawn back from the teeth in a grotesque grin. From some of the skulls still hung lank black hair.

The black hair, the darkness of the skin and the prominence of the cheek bones identified the dead to Hatfield. They were, he knew, Indians, doubtless the slaves held captive by the old Spaniards and forced to work the mine. Here they were kept locked up at night. For some reason they had been abandoned by their heartless captors to die a slow and torturing death by thirst and starvation. Doubtless a hundred years, and perhaps much more, had passed since they sat down to their last long sleep in the black dark.

Gulden held the lantern high, and gave an evil chuckle.

'Yuh'll have company while yuh're waitin' for the Boss,' he said. 'And I reckon these other hellions will have company while *they're* waitin' for Jedgment Day. Come over here!'

While the others stood alert and watchful, he picked up one of the clanking leg irons that showed signs of recent oiling and use, clamped it around Hatfield's ankle and locked it with a key he took from his pocket.

'You ain't the first one this has been used on,' he remarked, gesturing to a corner where something lay huddled. 'Over there is another jigger what got in the Boss's way, or what's left of him. He didn't last long.—He'd already been plugged—but you look purty husky. Reckon yuh'll be able to last quite a spell, even though yuh're liable to wish yuh couldn't. A feller gets thirsty mighty fast in here.'

The tall man gave an impatient exclamation. 'Cut the big medicine, Gull, and come along,' he ordered. 'Yuh're stayin' here in the hangout. Me and Parks are goin' to ride to meet the Boss. He'll be waitin' over to the forks to find out if we dropped the noose on this jigger before he decides whether to come over here or ride on south.'

They trooped out together, taking the lantern with them. Hatfield sat down in the dark, his chain clanking unpleasantly, fished out his tobacco and matches and rolled a cigarette. For some minutes he smoked, relishing the quieting effect of the tobacco, and thinking hard. He knew he was on a very tough spot and that his chances of getting off it were scant.

'Those hellions would never let me get out of here alive, after I've once seen their hole-up,' he told himself. 'Reckon what they were

75

looking for was that map. Lucky I stowed it away in my belt. That thing must be mighty important. They were evidently looking for it when they ransacked the mine office last night. They found the hunk of ore and took it along with them. Reckon they figured if I left the ore with Hodges, I would have left the map with him also. When they didn't find it, they decided I must have it. Now they don't know where it is, but are determined to find out. If I don't work out something in a hurry, it'll be curtains for me when the Boss, whoever in blazes he is, gets here. And I've a notion I haven't got much time.'

Pinching out his cigarette butt, he examined his fetters. The iron cuff fitted snugly about his leg just above the ankle bone. The chain, while rusty, was evidently firm enough. A tentative tug or two convinced him it was far beyond his strength to break. It was securely riveted to the upright bar and the bar was set deep in the stone of floor and ceiling.

He could hear Gulden banging about in the other room. Soon the smell of frying bacon and boiling coffee drifted into his prison. Gulden was evidently preparing a meal. After a while he quieted down save for an occasional rattle of knife and fork. Then a long silence ensued.

Hatfield rolled another cigarette. After lighting it, he held the burning match aloft and gazed about. The chain that held him, he saw, was about six feet in length, of stout links welded together. His eyes roved over the motionless mummies of the dead Indians. They centered on the scattering of picks and shovels and bars. One stout bar lay not far off. He felt he could reach it by stretching out on the floor. It would make an admirable weapon, were he free to use it. But it was useless so long as he was chained to the upright rod. The last flicker of the match showed the next rod in the row about three feet distant. Its image remained fixed on his retina for a moment after the light went out.

Suddenly he uttered a hoarse exclamation under his breath. That upright rod less than three feet distant—the chain, a good six feet in length—the stout iron bar within reach. His heart beat wildly with renewed hope as he listened intently for any sound of movement in the outer room. All was silent. Perhaps Gulden slept. Tingling with impatience and apprehension as he was, he decided to wait a little longer before putting the plan that had suddenly formulated in his brain into action. He was almost certain to make some noise. If Gulden heard he might get suspicious and come to investigate.

Slowly the minutes dragged past and the silence continued. Hatfield could stand it no longer. He resolved to take the chance. Very gently he moved the full length of his chain in the direction of the iron bar. He stretched out prone on the floor, groped about with fingers.

Finally his hand touched the rough, rounded surface of the bar. He gripped it, drew it to him. Then he got stealthily to his feet, careful to avoid clanking the chain. He gathered it up in his hands, stepped to the upright rod only a few feet distant. Carefully he walked around the rod, winding the chain about the stout upright. The length between the rod and the one to which it was riveted hung slightly slack.

Hatfield continued to walk about the rod, winding the chain around it, carefully stepping over the loosely hanging section between the two uprights. Finally he had nearly a dozen turns around the second rod. He stepped toward the first rod, drawing taut the end of the chain secured to the leg iron. Then he took a loop in the slack between the two rods, thrust the iron bar into the loop and twisted. This gave him a terrific leverage. The section of chain between the two rods tightened and hummed. Hatfield twisted the bar still more. In his strained position it was awkward to handle. The veins stood out on his forehead like cords. Sweat poured down his face. Great back and arm muscles writhed and bulged under his thin shirt, threatening to rip the fabric. He shook as with ague. The chain hummed, the uprights creaked and groaned.

Suddenly there was a sharp snap. The bar slipped in Hatfield's grip as the tension on it eased. A link had parted.

Hatfield put more pressure on the bar,

twisting with every atom of his strength. He felt the broken link stretch apart. Not daring to let the loose ends of the chain clatter on the rock floor, he eased off on the bar, ran trembling fingers along the chain until he found the snapped link. With a gasp of relief he realized the opening was wide enough to ease the companion link through. He laid down the bar and twisted the link with his fingers. The chain parted. He eased one end to the floor, deftly unwound the other length from about the upright. He was free! And there was no sound from Gulden!

He looped up the loose chain and wound it about his leg, knotting it as securely as possible, so it would not drag clanking on the floor when he moved. Then he picked up the bar that had been his salvation, paused a minute to catch his breath, then stole silently out of the prison chamber and along the tunnel on stockinged feet. He reached the outer room, peered cautiously into its lighted interior.

Gulden sat at the table, his back to the inner tunnel mouth, his chin sunk on his breast. He was undoubtedly drowsing. Hatfield stole out of the tunnel and entered the chamber, the bar gripped and ready. He raised it aloft.

And at that instant the length of chain looped around his leg slipped, fell to the floor with a clanking clatter.

Gulden leaped to his feet, whirled about, hand streaking to his gun. Hatfield leaped forward and struck.

The blow missed Gulden's arm, but it struck his drawn gun squarely, sending it spinning across the room. Hatfield whirled up the bar for a second blow.

Gulden dived under the blow with catlike swiftness. The bar whizzed harmlessly over his head. Hatfield's wrist crashed onto Gulden's shoulder. The force of the contact opened his fingers, the bar clanged to the floor. Before he could recover, Gulden's huge reaching hands fastened on his throat in a vice-like grip. Backward and forward the two men reeled in a silent death grapple.

Gulden, though nearly a foot shorter than the tall Ranger, was many pounds heavier, and he seemed to be made of steel wires. Hatfield battered at his head with his fists, but Gulden buried his face against the other's breast and grimly held on. Hatfield tore at his corded wrists but could not loosen the terrible grasp of his thick fingers. His lungs were bursting for want of air, his head was spinning. There seemed to be a red-hot iron band tightening and tightening about his chest. Before his bulging eyes formed a thin, oval-tinted mist. His strength was going. And still Gulden tightened his awful grip.

With the strength of desperation, Hatfield hurled himself backward. He struck the stone floor with a bone-wracking crash. At the same time he jerked down on Gulden's wrists with

80

every ounce of force in him, driving his leg, stiff as an iron rod, upward. The throttling fingers tore free from his throat. Gulden's body shot into the air. He howled with pain as he turned a complete somersault and hurtled downward, landing on his head, his body stretched out at an angle.

There was the thud of Gulden's skull on the stone, a sharp crack, then a queer, spasmodic tattoo of boot heels pounding the rock floor.

Hatfield staggered to his feet, gulping in great draughts of life-giving air. Reeling and swaying, he stared at Gulden, who lay on his stomach, his head twisted about at a horrid angle, so that his distorted face glared with fixed eyes over his right shoulder.

'Bust his neck when he landed!' Hatfield muttered between gasps for breath. A deadly nausea swept over him. He lurched to the wall and leaned against it, his head spinning, red flashes storming before his eyes, his muscles turning to water. For some minutes he sagged against the stone, until his brain cleared a little, his strength began to come back. Finally he straightened up, stood rocking on his feet a moment, then staggered to the table.

Retrieving his gun belts from where they lay, he buckled them on. He made sure that his long Colts were fully loaded and in perfect working condition. Then he turned Gulden over on his back, fumbled his pockets until he found the key to the leg iron and unlocked the

81

cuff. The chain rattled to the floor. Painfully he drew on his boots, recovered his possessions from the table and stowed them away.

Somebody had removed Goldys' rig, which lay nearby. Hatfield cinched with trembling fingers, located his Winchester and slid it into the saddle boot. The urgent necessity now was to get away before the Boss and his men arrived at the mine. Weak and shaken as he was, Hatfield knew he was in no shape for a desperate battle against overwhelming odds. He paused just long enough to turn out Gulden's pockets. He discovered nothing of any significance. Leading Goldy, he headed for the outer air. Getting into the saddle was considerable of a chore, but with the good horse between his thighs he felt much better.

Full dark had long since fallen and the brush flanked lane was black as pitch, but Hatfield sent Goldy along it at a good pace. Without slackening speed the sorrel crashed through the thin fringe of growth, Hatfield dimly saw the shapes of a group of horsemen directly in front of him and heading in his direction.

Somebody gave a yelp of alarm. Hatfield's voice rang out like a golden bugle call—

'Trail, Goldy! Trail!'

The great sorrel shot forward, his hoofs drumming the ground. And over his tossing head, Hatfield's guns blazed and thundered.

Yells of alarm split the air, and a howl of pain. Goldy struck one horse shoulder to shoulder and sent it sprawling to the ground. Hatfield's flailing gun barrel crunched against bone. Then they were through the whirling, demoralized tangle and flashing along the trail. Guns boomed behind them, lead hissed past, but a second later they were around the bend and out of range.

Swaying easily to the motion of the racing sorrel, Hatfield ejected the spent shells from his guns and replaced them with fresh cartridges. He chuckled as he glanced over his shoulder. Nobody was in sight, and a moment later he was around a second turn in the trail.

Hatfield had little fear of pursuit now, even if it were attempted. He had full confidence in Goldy's great speed and endurance. But nevertheless he was taking no chances. He did not slacken the sorrel's pace until he reached the point where the old track joined the Dead Star Trail many miles distant.

CHAPTER SEVEN

Meanwhile there was a wrathful gathering in the mine tunnel beneath the slope. The outlaws had removed their masks and were grouped around Gulden's dead body. One was bleeding from an ugly bullet gash in his cheek. A second had a deep cut in his scalp, a memento of the hardness of Hatfields' gun barrel. Only one

83

man had not uncovered his face, a very tall and broad man who paced up and down the room with long, smooth strides.

The tall, slender man was revealed as Walsh Knox, the Shanghai M foreman, his eyes glinting with anger, his aggressive tuft of beard bristling forward on his prominent chin.

'What I'd like to know,' Knox was saying, 'is how did that hellion bust this chain?'

'I don't know,' replied the masked man, 'unless you carelessly overlooked a weak link.'

'Weak link, hell!' barked Knox. 'Here's the link that was busted. The break's clean across and plumb fresh. That chain would have held a two-thousand-pound beef. But he busted it!'

'Busted Gulden's neck, too,' muttered one of the group around the body. 'I wouldn't have believed there was a man livin' who could do that. Gulden was a bull. There's folks what say that Ranger hellion ain't human. I'm beginnin' to think mebbe they're right.'

His companions glanced nervously at the speaker. The masked man gave a derisive snort.

'He's human all right,' he retorted. 'He's smart, that's all, too smart for you thick-heads. I'll take over the chore of looking after him next time, and you'll see whether he's human. You're sure he didn't have that map, Knox?'

'Plumb sure,' the other replied. 'We gave him a thorough combin', and found nothin'. He sure didn't have it on him.'

84

'I've a notion where it is,' the other growled. 'I'll attend to that later. What I can't understand is why you didn't first thing get hold of that map the other morning when you had the chance. You knew very well that double-crossing driver had it on him.'

Knox flushed, but met the other's hard eyes. 'I reckon we was just too anxious to see what was in the cart,' he replied. 'We didn't figger on bein' interrupted like we was.'

'Yes, you would do that,' the other said bitterly. 'Grab at a peso and let a fortune slip through your fingers. I don't know what's the matter with you of late. Tonight makes three chores you've bungled one after another. You didn't used to be like this.'

'Uh-huh, and mebbe I was never up against anythin' like I been of late,' growled Knox. 'I wish I'd done for that big hellion while I had the chance. I won't feel safe so long as he's amblin' around loose. I figger yuh made a mistake by tryin' to keep him outa this section in the first place. Yuh'd oughta know he wouldn't scare.'

'I never figured he'd scare,' the other replied quietly. 'I wrote that note to start him on a cold trail, to have him looking for the sort of person who would write that kind of a note. And I believe it worked.'

'Mebbe,' Knox agreed doubtfully, 'but he's been gettin' too damn close for comfort. But you ain't never fell down on anythin' yet, and I don't reckon yuh will this time no matter how loco things look.'

'I figger the hull business is damn foolishment,' growled one of the listening group. 'We're doin' purty well as it is. Why go sashayin' off after somethin' that may never amount to anythin' anyhow?'

The masked man whirled on him like a cat. His long arm shot out, his hand fastened on the speaker's throat and lifted him clear off his feet. With a strangled yell, the other went for his gun. Fingers like rods of steel clamped his wrist. He croaked with agony as his wrist bones ground together. The gun thudded to the floor. He clutched at the masked man's wrist with his free hand, but was powerless to free his throat from that throttling grip. His tongue protruded, his terror-glazed eyes bulged from his head as the grip tightened.

The masked man spoke, his voice quiet, unruffled—

'I should squeeze just a little harder. But I won't, not this time. You're getting one more chance, and the last. There won't be a second one for anybody else who questions my orders or my judgment. That goes for all of you.'

He loosened his grasp suddenly. The victim fell to the floor, groaning and retching. The masked man swept the group with his steady eyes. Under that baleful stare the owlhoots shifted their feet, glanced uneasily away. The masked man spoke again—

'All right now, you fellows scatter out of here. You've still got a chore to do tonight. Pack Gulden along with you. We don't want Tom Reeves to find him if he comes snooping around here, as he's liable to do as soon as that big hellion gets word to him of what happened. Knox, you're heading back to the Shanghai M.'

'It's a damn long ride, after all I've done today,' Knox grumbled.

'I know it is,' the other replied, adding significantly, 'but remember you're working for a cripple, and you have all the work of the spread on your hands. Tomorrow the other cowmen of the valley will be dropping in to arrange details of the roundup next week. It would look funny if you weren't on the job, especially as you are about certain to be chosen roundup boss. We're taking no chances on anything with that infernal Ranger mavericking around.'

Knox growled an oath but nodded agreement.

Ranchhouse and bunk-house were both dark when Hatfield reached the Lazy R headquarters. He stabled his horse, entered the house by way of the front door, which was unlocked, and gained his room without waking anybody. He undressed and stretched out wearily on his bed. Although he was very tired, he did not immediately go to sleep. For nearly an hour he lay thinking hard. He was just about to close his eyes when he heard the front door

87

open. Steps crossed the outer room and ascended the stairs. They died away for a moment, then resumed on the floor over Hatfield's head. He lay listening until the sound ceased. Then he turned over and closed his eyes.

'Looks like *Señor* Emory sort of made a night of it,' he told the darkness as he drifted off to sleep.

Hatfield awakened early. He found himself stiff and sore, and his throat was somewhat swollen; but he felt in good shape despite the hectic happenings of the previous night. Before leaving his room, he took the mysterious map from his secret belt pocket and eyed it with appreciation.

'I've a notion this thing is going to be sort of valuable to me,' he mused. 'Those sidewinders seem to set a heap of store by it, and I've a feeling they won't try to dry gulch me from ambush or anything like that until they get some notion of what I did with it. But if they ever get their hands on me again—gentlemen, hush!'

Hatfield had breakfast with Sharon, Grant Emory and the hands in the big dining room. The foreman had dark circles under his eyes and seemed somewhat preoccupied, but he was cheerful enough.

He was not cheerful a couple of hours later, however, when a young cowboy rode a lathered horse to the veranda where Emory sat familiarizing Hatfield with the general layout of the Lazy R spread. Emory descended the steps in answer to the puncher's call, and listened to what he had to say. When he returned, his face was angry and worried.

'What's the matter, Grant?' asked Sharon, who had come out at the sound of hoofbeats.

'They got another bunch last night, that's what,' Emory replied wrathfully. 'More than a hundred fat beefs from the southwest pasture.'

The girl looked grave. 'Grant,' she said, 'we can't stand much more of this with the obligations we have to meet.'

'I know we can't,' Emory returned gloomily, 'but what in blazes to do? They hit here, they hit there, and are gone like shadows inter a dark canyon. We can't set a guard on every beef that's amblin' the range.'

'How about guarding the lower end of the Dead Star Trail?' the girl suggested.

'Tom Reeves tried that,' Emory grunted. He spent three nights down there with a bunch of deputies. Hardly anybody knowed anythin' about it. And what happened? While he was there watchin', we lost a bunch, and so did the Scab Eight. And that infernal trail is supposed to be the only way across the desert to the River.'

'Could they head across the hills to the west and circle south?' Hatfield asked.

'Only up to the north,' Emory replied. 'To do that they'd have to drive across the Forked

S, the Wallop and the Shanghai M. They could never make it from our spread or the Scab Eight durin' the dark hours. If only the Shanghai M and the Fiddle-Back, up to the north, was losin' cows, that might explain it, but everybody's been losin' 'em. Nope, they must go south.'

'Why can't the desert be crossed except by way of the Dead Star Trail?'

'Faults—gulches—buttes. A horse can't hardly make it any place except by the trail, let alone a bunch of beefs in a hurry. Over west of the west range, there's nothin' to it. Easy goin' all the way south, but there's no gettin' across them hills with cows, except up north where the pass is. And no way at all across the Perdida Range, or across the desert southeast of it.'

Hatfield nodded, his eyes thoughtful, and relapsed into silence.

'Well, right now we've got other things to do,' Emory remarked. 'Hatfield, you might as well ride with me to the Fiddle-Back and the Shanghai M. You can meet some folks that way. I want to talk over the roundup next week with Ralph Adams, who owns the Fiddle-Back, and with Talbot Morrow over to the Shanghai M.'

A little later he and Hatfield saddled up and rode north. First they visited the Fiddle-Back. Adams, the owner, proved to be a crusty oldtimer with a vivid vocabulary of unusual profanity. Hatfield liked him immediately.

After discussing details with Adams, they rode west across the range to the Shanghai M *casa*.

Walsh Knox, the foreman, was on the veranda when they rode up to the ranchhouse. He gave them a cooly impersonal greeting, his lips twisting in a sneer as he spoke to Emory. He raised a slender hand and tugged at his chin tuft as Hatfield was introduced to him.

'Take a load off yore feet,' he invited. 'The Boss will be right out.'

Emory took a chair. Hatfield sat down on the edge of the porch, his long legs dangling, and leaned back comfortably against a post.

Knox stuck his head in the door and called an order. A moment later there was a sound of boots pounding the floor. Two husky punchers appeared packing a chair in which was seated Talbot Morrow, a blanket resting across his knees. The cowboys placed the chair on the veranda and retired.

Morrow gave Hatfield a steady look from his blue eyes and acknowledged his introduction in a deep and not unpleasant voice. He shook hands with a firm grip. Hatfield resumed his seat on the edge of the porch and listened while Emory and the Shanghai M owner discussed with Knox the details of the coming roundup. Suddenly his gaze fixed on Morrow's well polished boots that rested supinely on the floor, held for an instant, then glanced away. He fished out the makin's and rolled a cigarette, his black brows drawing together until the concentration furrow was deep between them.

CHAPTER EIGHT

By hard riding, Hatfield and Emory reached the Lazy R in time for a late supper. After eating, while Emory discussed the roundup with Sharon in the living room, Hatfield strolled out for a look at the night. When he mounted the veranda steps, some time later, he paused for a moment. Through the open window he could view the interior of the living room. Sharon had evidently gone upstairs. Grant Emory was in the act of taking a book from the shelf of technical works. He sat down, opened the book and became absorbed in its contents. When Hatfield entered the room, he was so intent on his reading that he merely glanced up in the detached way of a man whose train of thought has been broken, waved his hand in greeting and immediately dropped his eyes to the printed page.

Hatfield passed to his own room, his face thoughtful.

The following day Hatfield rode the range with Emory and the Lazy R punchers, getting the lowdown on the holdings. That evening, while Emory was busy with some chores, he sat in the living room and talked with Sharon. In the course of the conversation, the girl made some remark concerning her father.

'You say your dad died not long ago?' Hatfield asked.

'Yes,' the girl replied quietly, but with bitterness in her soft voice. 'A little more than three months ago he—was murdered.'

'Murdered?'

'Yes.'

'Any notion who killed him?'

'I'm sure I saw the man who did it,' Sharon replied slowly, 'but nobody has seen him since.'

'How was that?'

'Dad rode home from town one night,' the girl replied. 'With him was a man he introduced to me as Burt Avery, a prospector. He was an old man with gray hair and a great gray beard. He was dressed very roughly, his clothes patched and faded. He and Dad sat talking until late at night. I don't know what about. Early the next morning they rode off together, west across the range. Dad told me he would be back before dark. When night came he wasn't back, and he wasn't back the next morning. Naturally the boys went looking for him. They found his body over on the west range, beside a spring. He had been shot in the back of the head. The sheriff hunted for the prospector, but did not find him. Nobody has seen him or heard anything of him.'

'Was your dad robbed?'

The girl shook her head. 'No, he was not.

What money he carried was still in his pocket, as was his watch. It was very sad, and very strange. Dad never had an enemy that anybody ever heard of. Why that prospector should have killed him is beyond understanding. In fact, of late I have wondered if it could possibly have been an accident. Such things have happened, you know. Perhaps the prospector accidentally shot him, and became frightened and ran away.'

'Could be,' Hatfield admitted.

Sharon's blue eyes were starry with tears. Instinctively Hatfield laid a comforting hand on hers. She clutched at his fingers as a child would. They sat in silence, hand in hand, busy with their thoughts.

And Grant Emory chose that instant to enter the room. Hatfield and Sharon, their backs to him, did not hear his quiet entrance.

For a moment, Emory stood without speaking, his hands balling into trembling fists, his eyes glittering. But almost instantly the gleaming eyes clouded, dulled. He drew a deep breath, and seemed to arrive at a sudden decision. He eased back a step, then moved forward noisily.

Hatfield and Sharon turned at the sound, their hands falling apart. Emory's lips twisted in a smile that never reached his tortured eyes. He held up a long sheet of paper upon which words and figures were scrawled in a rude schoolboy hand.

94

'Sharon,' he said, 'I've been chekin' the stores we got. There's a heap of stuff we're goin' to need for next week. I've made out a list. I've got a hatful of chores to do tomorrow, so I wonder if you couldn't ride up to town and have Vanstaver, the storekeeper, send this stuff down to us.'

'Of course I will, Grant,' the girl replied. 'I'll start early.'

Emory nodded, seemed to hesitate. 'Hatfield,' he said at length, 'would you mind ridin' along with her? I got a funny feelin' of late about havin' her ride the range alone, because of what all's been happenin' in the section of late, I reckon. Mebbe I'm loco, but just the same I can't help feelin' that way.'

'Be glad to,' Hatfield agreed instantly. 'Funny things appear to be going on hereabouts, all right. I figure you got a good notion.'

Hatfield and the girl headed for town the following morning. The air was cool and crisp with the first touch of autumn. Frost gleamed on the grass heads, catching the sunlight in a jewelled sheen. Already the long slopes of the hills were touched with gold and scarlet, and leaves like-flecks of flame floated down as a gentle wind stirred the branches. Overhead the Texas sky was deeply blue, but a mystic purple haze shrouded the crests of the mountains and misted the thin fine line of the horizon. Nature was weaving a shroud for the dying year, and

95

brightening its somber gray with the rainbowed promise of new birth when the sunlight would once more turn from white to gold and the tender green of Spring would tip the leaden monotone of the leafless branches. Everywhere was the beauty of approaching death and decay, which is as fair to the seeing eye and the understanding heart as is the glory of up-springing life.

The man and the girl who rode together felt its truth and were silent—silent with the appreciation of the loveliness all about them. More than once the blue-eyed girl glanced a trifle wistfully at the sternly handsome profile of the man who rode beside her. But suddenly her red lips quirked at the corners and the blue eyes danced with laughter.

Hatfield abruptly came out of his preoccupation. 'What you laughing at, Sharon?' he asked wonderingly.

'I was just thinking, Jim,' she replied, using his given name for the first time, 'of the philosopher who searched the world over for the jewel of happiness, looking afar, dreaming dreams of the impossible, ever seeking, only to find when, old and disillusioned, he wandered home once more, that all the time it had lain in plain view by his own doorstep.'

Hatfield smiled down at her from his great height, and his strangely colored eyes were all kindness.

'Too many folks never learn that lesson,

Sharon,' he said. 'It isn't often that anyone as young as you even senses it. I figure you're lucky.'

'Yes,' she replied softly, 'but just the same, it's something to have dreamed!'

When they arrived at town Sharon immediately contacted Vanstavern, the keeper of the general store. The chores she had to do would occupy her the rest of the day. Hatfield dropped in for a talk with Sheriff Reeves. He found old Tom morose and irritable. He swore gloomily upon hearing of the widelooped cattle, and exclaimed in astonishment and wrath when Hatfield recounted his experience in the old mine tunnel.

'Reckon I'd better head down there and look the place over?' he asked.

Hatfield shook his head. 'Don't see as there would be any sense to it,' he replied, 'taking a sixty-mile ride for nothing. They undoubtedly cleared out of there pronto, and took what was left of Gulden with them. Figure you wouldn't find anything when you got there.'

The sheriff knit his brows. 'I sort of rec'lect seein' a jigger of that hellion's general description hangin' around town of late,' he remarked. 'But we get a lot of mavericks here from time to time, so I reckon it don't mean much.'

A sudden thought seemed to strike him. 'By the way, feller, where did you come from and what brought yuh to this section?' he asked.

Hatfield's rather wide mouth quirked at the corners. He did not immediately reply, but sat studying the old peace officer's lined face for several moments. He had already decided that Reeves was honest and trustworthy, although not overly supplied with intelligence. He felt also that he could be depended upon to keep his mouth shut. Abruptly he arrived at a decision. His hand dropped to the secret pocket in his broad leather belt. A moment later he laid something on the table between them.

Sheriff Reeves stared at the object, his jaw sagging. It was a gleaming *silver star set on a silver circle*, the feared and honored badge of the Texas Rangers!

'Good gosh!' the sheriff exploded. 'Yuh're a Ranger! McDowell sent yuh over here?' Suddenly his eyes blazed. He stared at Hatfield.

'And, by gosh, I know yuh!' he exclaimed. 'I got yuh placed now. Yuh're the Lone Wolf!'

'Been called that,' Hatfield admitted.

Sheriff Reeves stared, almost in awe, at the man whose exploits were becoming legend throughout the Southwest.

'The Lone Wolf!' he repeated. 'Settin' right here in my office! Well, if this don't take the hide off a double-branded beef!'

Hatfield chuckled, but immediately became grave. 'Yes,' he said, 'Captain McDowell sent me over here, to try and get a line on Quantrell,

98

but so far it's principally been Quantrell getting a line on me. He's a salty proposition with brains.'

'Uh-huh, whoever he is, he's got plenty of wrinkles on his horns,' the sheriff agreed. 'Got any kind of a lead on him?'

'I have a notion,' Hatfield replied slowly, 'but I haven't much to go on, yet. By the way, there seems to be bad blood between Grant Emory and Knox, the Shanghai M foreman. How come?'

'That's a funny thing,' the sheriff replied reflectively. 'When Knox showed up here with Tal Morrow, about six months back, him and Emory got real chummy. Were pardin' around together a heap. Reckon they found considerable in common. Emory used to be a wild sort of young hellion. Gambled a heap, drank considerable. Flashy temper, lightnin' fast with his gun hand. That was before Weston Remington got cashed in and Emory took over at the Lazy R. Since then he's been mighty steady. Responsibility, I reckon. About that time he 'peared to break with Knox. Knox used to visit the Lazy R frequent. He don't any more. Uh-huh, they used to be plumb thick, but now they seem to go out of the way to show they ain't got no use for each other.'

'Go out of the way to show it?' Hatfield repeated thoughtfully.

'Uh-huh, they're plumb on the prod against each other. Wouldn't be surprised if they had a showdown some time. They're both salty propositions. Between you and me, I think they're both sweet on Miss Sharon.'

'And that explains quite a few things,' Hatfield observed with understanding. 'Knox came here with Morrow, I believe you said.'

'That's right. He was Morrow's foreman over in Arizona. Morrow owned a spread over there. He sold out and came to take over the Shanghai M, which is the biggest and best outfit in the valley when his Dad passed in his chips. Pity about him gettin' crippled up. He always was a big, up-standin' fine lookin' feller. I rec'lect him when he left the section. Wasn't but a boy in them days, but was already plenty hefty. Wanted to see the world, he said. Roamed around considerable, I take it. Then he sort of settled down in Arizona. Wrote to his Dad regular. I recollect when the word come, a coupla years back, that he'd got shot and crippled. The news plumb broke up old Arn Morrow. He wanted Tal to come home then, but Tal calc'lated to hang on over west. An independent sort of cuss. Of course, when his Dad took the Big Jump he came back to look after the property here which was evidently a heap sight more valuable than his holdin's in Arizona.'

Hatfield, who had listened intently to the sheriff's story, nodded.

'Reeves,' he said abruptly, 'there's no telegraph office here, I take it?'

'Nope. One at Dorantes, the railroad town.

Why?'

'I want to send a message to McDowell,' Hatfield replied. 'Give me a pen and paper and I'll write it out now. I want you to see it. I'll have the answer come addressed to you.'

Reeves produced pen and paper. Hatfield wrote a carefully worded message to the Ranger Captain. Reeves read it and his eyes glowed.

'By gosh, yuh may have somethin' there!' he exclaimed. 'I've had a funny notion or two about that galoot myself. As I said before, he's a salty proposition.'

Hatfield smiled, and changed the subject. 'Now about getting to Dorantes,' he suggested.

'It's a forty-mile ride, mebbe a little more,' the sheriff said. 'Yuh take the road east till yuh hit the Dead Star Trail at the salt flats. It's nearly twenty miles to the flats, and another twenty miles or so across the flats and the hills to the north. Keep your eyes skun for Quantrell and his bunch,' he added half jokingly. 'They've raised hell on that trail.'

CHAPTER NINE

Bidding Reeves tell Sharon he had a chore to do and would see her in the morning, Hatfield rode east out of Gavilan. Across the rangeland the going was easy and he made good time, but it was different when he reached the flats. Here was a land of desolation and decay, the blinding surface of the salt stretching for miles, with the Dead Star Trail writhing like a tortured snake across the blasted salt. The heat was terrific and the fine powder stirred by blasts of a sultry wind parched Hatfield's lips and caused his eyes to smart unbearably. On all sides, weird looking dunes started up, misty and unreal in the distance, advancing, retreating, seeming to fade away and vanish only to reappear with startling distinctness through the vagaries of refracted light.

The surface of the trail was firm enough, although at times deeply silted by the sifting salt, but it was different away from its tortuous course. The place was a veritable plain of the white shadow of death. The surface was covered with little dimples and cones that made walking almost impossible, with here and there perfectly smooth reaches glistening like powdered ice. Once, moved to examine closer a strikingly shaped dune, Hatfield sent Goldy out onto such a surface. Almost instantly the surface trembled and heaved under his weight. Behind him he left tracks just as plainly in the salt as if they had been imprinted in snow. The substance that looked so utterly dry was wet and sticky. A moment later, one hoof broke through the shallow crust.

Hatfield jerked Goldy sharply back. Through the hoof break oozed water that looked like acid. Reining the sorrel carefully about, he returned to the trail, which he did not leave again. His glance swept the scene of stark desolation with understanding. The grip of his imagination rolled back the ages and he visioned what this ominous terrain once had been. Here between the battlements of the hills that were its shores, heaved and tossed a shallow lake. Strange and mighty monsters, scaled and tailed, prowled and fed and fought amid the reeds under a blazing reddish sun. Other monsters soared over the dark water on webbed, membranous wings, snapping their teeth-filled, rat-trap beaks at insects whizzing past in the hot, steamy air. The growth that fringed the lake was unbelievably luxuriant in its lush green, but the hills beyond were naked, heat scorched rock. It was a raw, unfinished, terrible and forbidding landscape of earth's youngness. In Hatfield's ears rang an agonized scream as the greater dragon pinned the lesser amid the slime. Before his eyes floated glimpses of the endless, numberless tragedies that accompanied progressing life in the slow climb up the ladder of the eons. Life that changed and developed as the mountains heaved and sank and the waters of the vast lake dried to stagnant pools that deposited their silt upon its dessicated bed. While the hills eroded, the naked stone became surfaced with fertile earth and the green that had been the border of the ancient lake wrapped the hills instead in its emerald mantle to form a jewelled setting for the white plain of death across which the Ranger rode.

'And the day will come again when all this will be changed once more,' he mused, 'when the hills will have worn down to nothingness under the ceaseless caress of the fingers of time, when this which looks like eternal death will once more bud and burgeon with renewed life.'

The thought was inspiring amid the forbidding scene and he faced the soaring hills that swiftly drew nearer, with a smile.

Nevertheless he heaved a sigh of relief when he finally left the flats and began climbing the slopes. Not that the road through the hills did not leave much to be desired. It was still the Dead Star Trail, and the Dead Star Trail seemed to always seek out the most sinister terrain for its endless windings. Soon Hatfield found himself riding along the edge of a beetling precipice that dropped hundreds of feet to a canyon floor, with a rugged cliff forming the inner wall of the trail. The turns were frequent and sharp, the rise very steep. He raised his head suddenly as a clicking of hoofs and a rumbling sounded somewhere ahead. A moment later a bulky stagecoach, rocking and swaying in its cradle of springs, lurched around a turn and bore down upon him.

As Hatfield reined aside to let the equipage

pass, he noted that two men with ready rifles paced their horses on either side of the coach. They favored Hatfield with hard, searching glances as they passed, but nodded a greeting. A moment later a turn farther down the trail hid them from view.

'Must be a payroll or a gold shipment in that coach,' the Ranger mused as he continued on his way. 'Those jiggers sure look ready for trouble.'

Half an hour later he uttered a sharp exclamation. The trail ahead seemed to leap abruptly off into space. As he drew nearer, however, he saw that it made an almost right-angled turn around a bulge of cliff.

Goldy took the turn on gingerly placed hoofs. Hatfield glanced into the dark depths almost beneath his elbow and shook his head.

'Anything taking this bend at faster than a walk, coming down hill, wouldn't stop till it hit the bottom of the canyon in splinters,' he told the sorrel with conviction.

For a little over a mile more he rode without mishap. The turns were still frequent, but shallower, easier to negotiate. Not far to the front the crest of a rise stood out with knife-edge sharpness against the skyline. Goldy was toiling up the rise when Hatfield was startled by a stutter of shots somewhere beyond the crest. While he was wondering what they could mean, there was a pounding of hoofs, a roaring of wheels and a ponderous freight wagon drawn by four maddened horses swept over the ridge and thundered down the trail. In a fleeting glimpse before he whirled Goldy, Hatfield saw that the driver's seat was unoccupied, and that over the back of the seat a man's leg, around which the reins were wrapped, stuck stiffly into the air.

For the moment Hatfield did not have time to look for more. He was too busy putting some distance between himself and the juggernaut crashing toward him. But as Goldy easily held his own in the race, he turned in his saddle and stared back with narrowing eyes.

'That jigger who toppled off the seat may not be dead,' he told the sorrel, 'but he sure will be if that contraption tries to round the hairpin turn down below without slowing up. Feller, I reckon we got to try and do something about it. Hug that cliff, now, and we'll see what's what. We're liable to get squashed against the rock, but we got to take the chance.'

He slowed the sorrel's pace. The wagon quickly gained. As it drew near, Hatfield estimated its rate of speed and quickened Goldy's gait correspondingly. Soon the tossing heads of the runaway team were level with the sorrel's flank. As Hatfield surmised they would, the wagon team shied away from the golden horse a little. Hatfield swung one leg over the saddle and stood in his left stirrup. He let the wagon gain a little more, until the high seat was directly opposite. Holding Goldy's speed equal to that of the team, he estimated the distance and leaped. His clutching hands gripped the iron railing around the seat. He hung for an instant, his feet banging against the spinning front wheel, then by a prodigious muscular effort drew himself up and clambered onto the seat. With lightning swiftness he unwound the reins from about the leg protruding over the back of the seat. From the tail of his eye he saw that the leg belonged to a man who lay on his back on the heaped sacks of something in the wagon's bed. The man's face was covered with blood, but he was rolling his head from side to side in returning consciousness. A second man lay on his back, a blue hole between his staring eyes.

Hatfield shoved the leg out of the way, tightened the reins and put forth his strength. For minutes his efforts appeared to have not the slightest effect on the racing horses, and the hairpin turn was leaping to meet them with alarming speed. Gradually, however, the Ranger's iron strength began to tell. The horses floundered a little, their gait became broken. But now the turn was less than two hundred yards distant.

Hatfield put forth every ounce of force in his body. His great fear was that the reins might snap under the strain. Then it would indeed be curtains. But the heavy straps held. The horses slowed to a jolting trot, a walk. With the turn scarce a score of feet distant, they came to a halt and stood blowing and panting and rolling frightened eyes, but with all the 'run' taken out of them.

Behind Hatfield a voice was calling thickly. He turned, and saw the bloody-faced man on his knees gripping a rifle with trembling hands.

'Look out, feller,' he gasped hoarsely, 'them hellions are right on top of us.'

Hatfield leaned over the seat and snatched the rifle from him even as the sound of racing hoofs reached his ears. An instant later a group of masked men bulged around a turn less than a hundred yards to the rear.

Hatfield did not hesitate. The rifle leaped to his shoulder, spat fire and smoke. One of the riders reeled sideways with a yell of pain. The speeding horses were suddenly jerked back on their haunches. Hatfield fired again, saw the leg of a second man fly from the stirrup, and heard another agonized bellow. He fired a third time, and scored a miss. A scattering of wild shots answered him. Lead whined past. But, sheltered behind the high wagon seat, he did not offer much of a target. As he lined sights a fourth time, a voice bellowed orders. The group whirled their horses and went skalleyhootin' back around the turn. Hatfield sent a couple more slugs hissing after them, then lowered the smoking rifle.

The man in the back of the wagon was sitting up on the bulging sacks, looking rather sick and shaky, but apparently not much the worse for the bullet crease along the side of his head.

'Feller,' he said thickly, 'I'm sure obliged, plumb obliged. I never seed anythin' what looked as good as you did when you come climbin' onto that seat. I was just gettin' senses back, but I couldn't move or do a thing. I sure figgered I was a goner, like poor Jess here. Think those sidewinders will come back?'

Hatfield shook his head as he slipped over the seat and proceeded to bandage the other's wound with a handkerchief.

'Reckon they still are trying to figure what happened,' he replied. 'No, they wouldn't risk a chance coming back around that bend. They'd expect too hot a reception. The odds are all against them, and they know it. What in blazes is this all about? Since when have owlhoots taken to drygulching freight wagons in this section.'

The man hesitated, appeared to make up his mind about something.

'Reckon you got a right to know,' he said, 'and if yuh hanker to grab it off, I figger yuh've earned it,' he added with a wan grin. 'The Harqua Mine payroll money is under them sacks—nigh onto twenty thousand dollars in gold.'

Hatfield stared at him. 'I met the stage coming down trail a little while ago,' he remarked. 'It was guarded.'

The other nodded. 'Uh-huh, that was to fool Quantrell. It didn't fool him. Nothin' ever fools that sidewinder. The stage went through without any trouble. But when we came along with the wagon, Quantrell knowed the money was in it, don't ask me how. Him and his bunch throwed down on Jess and me. Plugged us both, but the horses got scairt at the shootin' and bolted. This wagon load looks heavy, but ain't. Nothin' but bran in them sacks. The bronks didn't pay it no mind when they decided to git up and git. Before them owlhoots could get down off the ridge where they were holed up—the cliffs end just over the rise—the bronks had a head start.'

Hatfield nodded. 'Somebody in the Quantrell outfit sure is in the know,' he commented thoughtfully, more to himself than to his companion. 'Well,' he continued, 'figure you can take this shebang into town alone? The sheriff should be notified, and you want the doctor to patch up your head.'

'I can take 'er in,' the other replied. 'I'm the driver. Poor Jess was supposed to be my leader. The rifle was hid under the sacks.'

'Lucky it was,' Hatfield replied. 'Mine is on my horse over there, and it would have been long shooting with sixes. Lucky, too, those reins tangled about your leg when you fell. Looks like you sort of got the breaks.'

'And the biggest one was you comin' along when yuh did, feller,' the driver declared with great heartiness. 'You goin' to ride on to Dorantes? Ain't yuh scairt them sidewinders

110

might be layin' for yuh?'

'Not much chance,' Hatfield returned. 'I've a notion they figured I was one of the stage coach guards come back to see what was going on and that the rest of those salty looking jiggers might not be far behind. No, I reckon they hightailed and kept sifting sand. Okay, I'll get my horse. You head for town.'

Despite his assuring words to the wagon driver, Hatfield was very much on the alert during the rest of his ride. However, he reached the railroad town without further incident and sent the message to Captain McDowell. He ate and headed back to Gavilan, arriving at the mining town at daylight. He and Goldy were both pretty well worn out by the excitement and the eighty-mile amble, but suffered nothing that a few hours of rest wouldn't right.

CHAPTER TEN

Sharon's chores took considerably more time than they had anticipated, keeping her busy all the following morning and part of the afternoon. Then, while they were eating before starting back to the ranch, a sudden rainstorm came up with a torrential downpour that lasted nearly an hour before the skies cleared. As a result, the sun was well down in the west before they finally got under way.

They rode at a good pace along the muddy trail. They passed the Shanghai M ranchhouse and continued for several miles. Here the trail curved slightly, running along the edge of a steep, brush grown slope that fell away to the right. On the left was open prairie, with scattered clumps of thicket near the trail. They were passing one of these when a slight rustling of brush in the thicket jerked Hatfield's head around. There was the ringing crack of a rifle. Jim Hatfield threw up his arms and pitched sideways from the saddle. He hit the slope beyond the edge of the trail, rolled down it, arms and legs thrashing, crashed through a bristle of growth and vanished.

Sharon Remington screamed chokingly, then stared with dilated eyes at three masked figures that rode out of the nearby thicket, rifles ready, the muzzle of one still wisping smoke.

'Stay put, Ma'am,' a voice called harshly. 'Don't want to hafta plug yuh, but we will if yuh try to run.'

In another instant his grip was on the girl's bridle. His companions, peered cautiously down the slope, from which came no sound or movement.

'Don't worry about him,' Sharon's captor called. 'When I line sights on a jigger, I don't miss. I got him square between the eyes. Didn't yuh see the way he went outa the hull? Only a jigger plugged in the head falls that way.'

'Mebbe we'd better go down and make sure,' one of his companions suggested doubtfully.

'We ain't wastin' no time,' the other growled. 'This is a travelled trail, and there's still more'n a hour of daylight. Want a bunch of cowhands to run inter us with this gal in tow? Come on, get goin'. Alf, catch that yaller horse.'

One of the men started to obey. He reached for Goldy's bridle.

There was a scream of rage, a flash of milk-white teeth and the man dodged back, howling. Blood streamed from his lacerated hand. Goldy whirled, streaked away into the thicket, curses and bullets volleying after him as he vanished from view. A moment later hoofs thudded north along the muddy trail.

Half unconscious and completely paralyzed by the terrific blow of the bullet on his skull, Hatfield lay beneath a screening brush far down the slope. Dimly he heard the shooting at his horse, then the thud of receding hoof beats. Instinctively he catalogued their direction—to the north. Then his senses left him.

Hatfield's awakening was painful. He was sore and bruised all over and his head ached abominably. But there was no limb that would not function, no joint that would not bend. Thankfully he realized, as he raised a trembling hand to his bloody head, that his wound was but a slight crease just above the right temple.

'But if I hadn't heard that brush snap and

113

jerked my head around just as the hellion pulled trigger, I'd have got it dead center,' he muttered. 'Looks like I was sorta off-trail when I figured having that map would keep the sidewinders from drygulching me. 'Pears they have other notions.'

He got to his feet, his strength quickly returning, and clawed his way up the slope. He was consumed with anxiety over what might have happened to Sharon.

He reached the trail, glared about. There was no one in sight, but tracks plainly scored in the muddy surface of the trail led north. As he stared at them, a plaintive whinny sounded. Goldy was peering from the shelter of the thicket. Hatfield gave a sharp whistle and the big sorrel trotted to him and nuzzled his hand.

'Couldn't drop a loop on you, feller, could they?' Hatfield exclaimed thankfully. 'Well, that's mighty lucky, 'cause you and I have work to do.'

He forked the sorrel, settled himself in the saddle. His face was set in lines bleak as chiselled granite, his eyes were coldly gray. He glanced at the sun, which was just touching the tips of the western crags, estimated the period of daylight that remained. He knew he could have been unconscious for but a little while, but long enough to let the owlhoots and their captives get a head start.

'And they know just where they're going, and I don't,' he muttered. 'They'll hightail it, and

I'll be slowed down by watching their trail. They're headed for somewhere in the west hills, sure as shooting, and if it goes dark on me before I find out just where, they'll give me the slip.'

He headed Goldy along the trail at a fast clip, for the hoof prints were so deeply scored in the soft surface that only an occasional glance was necessary to assure him that he was on the right track. For more than two miles the prints held to the trail, then they abruptly swerved to the left across the prairie, cutting toward the dark loom of the hills. Here the going was more difficult, but the rain drenched soil still held the marks plainly enough for the keen eyes of the Lone Wolf to discern them.

But now the sun was behind the western crags. The mountain crests were aflame with strange and glorious fires, but dark shadows swatched their slopes and were already creeping across the rangeland. Hatfield's black brows drew together and his lips tightened. There was just one thing in his favor. The owlhoots, undoubtedly convinced that the shot which hurled him from the saddle had been a fatal one, made no attempt to cover their trail. Finally, however, he was forced to dismount and proceed on foot, bending low over the sodden grass to see the crushed blades that alone showed the marks of passing hoofs. Despair was settling its cold blanket over him when the trail suddenly turned due west toward a dark canyon mouth.

Hatfield drew a deep breath of relief. The canyon was narrow with almost perpendicular towering walls. So long as they followed the gorge, the owlhoots could only forge straight ahead. He took a chance and forked Goldy again, and rode between the stony walls.

The floor of the canyon was rocky, grown with scattering brush of no great height, but its crowding walls forbade any turning aside by the quarry. Hatfield began to seriously estimate the lead they might be holding and to consider the danger of too close an approach.

Then abruptly the canyon forked. Hatfield pulled up with a muttered oath, dropped from the saddle and went down on hands and knees. Back and forth he covered the ground, his face close to the stony soil. There was still a little light in the sky, and the dregs of it seeped into the gorge. But nowhere could he find a trace of horses' irons to tell which fork of the canyon held his quarry. Then, when he was about ready to take a gamble at following the main canyon westward, he found what he was seeking. A little ways down the fork that veered to the south, he saw a broken branch dangling from a bush. The break was clean and fresh, the leaves of the twig still unwilted.

'Busted off by a horse brushing against it,' he muttered exultantly. He mounted once more and rode down the left fork, slowly now, for the sky was completely dark and only the shimmer of starlight filtered a ghostly glow into the gorge.

Suddenly he pulled Goldy to a halt. Somewhere ahead was a faint clicking, the beat of fast hoofs on the hard soil. Hatfield's mind worked at lightning speed. The sound told him that a single horseman was advancing up-canyon. He slipped to the ground, herded Goldy behind a bristle of growth, and waited. He drew his gun as the horseman drew near. But when the shadowy shape of the mounted man outlined against the sky, he held his fire.

'There were three of them—easy to tell that by the prints back there on the trail,' he told himself. 'That means that two are somewhere down this crack with Sharon. This jigger is heading for somewhere outside—doubtless to fetch the rest of the bunch, or to notify somebody they pulled off their chore. Downing him won't help matters and will just serve to warn the two hanging onto Sharon.

Standing tense and silent, he watched the horseman slog by. Not until the clicking had died away up the canyon did he risk an advance. He rode very slowly, so that the beat of Goldy's hoofs would be at a minimum. He had covered nearly a mile more and was considering proceeding on foot when suddenly he sniffed sharply. There was an undoubted tang of wood smoke in the air.

'Getting close,' he muttered, and halted the sorrel.

The canyon had widened somewhat and the low bushes nearer its mouth had been replaced by tall and thick growth. Hatfield forced Goldy into a thicket and tethered him.

'You stay here and keep quiet till I show up,' he told the sorrel. 'I won't be long, the chances are, if I come back at all. If I don't you can bust the bridle and look out for yourself.'

He proceeded cautiously on foot. The smell of smoke grew stronger. He pushed through a final fringe of brush and paused. Directly ahead was a shallow clearing, and not a hundred yards distant was a glowing square of yellow light with something dark and bulky looming behind it.

Hatfield quickly identified the glow as the light from a window in the wall of a roughly built cabin set close to the brush that grew along the eastern canyon wall. From its stick-and-mud chimney rose a spiral of smoke.

'They're in there,' he muttered exultantly. 'Those hellions must have more hangouts than a badger. This is a regular hole-in-the-wall country.'

As the starlight strengthened a trifle, he was able to make out details. The closed door of the cabin faced toward the west wall of the canyon. He considered the situation. To advance across the clearing would be altogether too risky. If anybody was watching out the window, they would be sure to spot him before he could reach the building. He began to edge along the growth, carefully keeping in its shadow.

'If that shack just has a back door, I've got a chance,' he told himself.

He reached the growth back of the cabin, stole forward with cautious steps. Soon he was directly behind the shack and but a few paces distant. Exultantly he realized that there was a back door, and, what was more, it stood slightly ajar, as a thin streamer of light evidenced. Taking a chance, he slipped a little nearer, peering and listening. To his ears came the sound of footsteps on the board flooring, and of harsh voices. Somewhere nearby a tethered horse stamped impatiently. He debated a quick dash for the partly open door, but regretfully shook his head.

'Couldn't do it without making some noise, and my eyes would be dazzled for a second by the light. If those two sidewinders happened to be both facing the back door, it would be too bad. Besides, Sharon might be right in my line of fire. No, I've got to get those jiggers to the window or the front door somehow. With their attention on the front of the cabin and their backs to this door, I'll have a chance.'

Slipping back to the growth, he cautiously but swiftly made his way through it until he reached a point almost opposite the cabin window, which was set in the side wall near the front of the shack. He wormed his way deeper into the brush and began gathering dry twigs and branches, carefully selected such as had

119

not been drenched by the recent rain. He worked at top speed, for there was no telling how soon the third man would return, doubtless with reinforcements. Soon he had a sizeable pile of dry wood heaped beneath a bush. With his knife he smoothed and levelled one side of a thick branch. This he carefully balanced on top of the pile. On the flat surface of the branch he laid two cartridges taken from his belt. Then he struck a match and set fire to the heap.

The smaller twigs at the bottom burned briskly, the flames licking upward. With a final glance at his handiwork, Hatfield turned and sped swiftly back to the rear of the cabin. He reached it without mishap, drew as near the door as he dared and crouched alert and expectant. Inside he could hear the movements of the two owlhoots, and their rumbling voices. Evidently they were preparing a meal. Nerves strained to the breaking point, he waited, and nothing happened. Had the cartridges rolled from the limb and bounced away from the fire? It began to look like it. He straightened up a trifle, to ease his cramped muscles, drew his guns and tensed for the dash to the cabin door he would have to risk, after all.

Startlingly loud in the silent night, a sharp report sounded from the edge of the clearing. Almost instantly it was followed by another.

Hatfield heard the owlhoots' startled exclamations and the pound of their boots as they dashed for the window. He lunged forward, covered the distance to the back door on flying feet and hit it with the point of his shoulder. It flew wide open with a crash, banging against the cabin wall. Narrowing his eyes against the light, Hatfield saw the two owlhoots crouching low by the window through which they were cautiously peering. They surged erect and whirled as the door banged open. Instantly the cabin seemed to explode with the roar of six-shooters.

Seconds later, one sleeve shot to ribbons, blood trickling from a bullet burn on his left hand, Hatfield lowered his smoking guns and stared through the fog at the two forms sprawled on the cabin floor.

'Reckon they're through hooting for good,' he muttered as he holstered his Colts and whirled about.

Sharon Remington lay on a bunk built against the far wall. Her wrists and ankles were loosely bound. With a couple of sweeps of his knife, Hatfield freed her. He raised her to a sitting position and she clung to him, shuddering convulsively. Her face was haggard, her eyes red from weeping.

'Oh, Jim,' she sobbed, 'I thought you were dead!'

'Not yet,' he told her. 'Reckon I take considerable killin'. Just lost a patch of hide off my head. Come on, honey, pull yourself together, we got to get out of here pronto. No telling when we'll have company we don't want.'

Taking time only to examine the bodies of the dead owlhoots who were hard-faced, unsavoury looking characters with nothing to single them out, Jim led her from the cabin. He quickly located her horse tied with those of the two owlhoots under a lean-to on the far side of the cabin.

'Up with you,' he told her. 'You're in no shape for walking.'

Taking the bridle, he headed back up the canyon, the led horse ambling along behind him. A few minutes later and he was mounted on Goldy and then they were riding swiftly out of the gorge.

It was nervous going until they reached the open rangeland. Hatfield hated to think of meeting the whole Quantrell bunch in the narrow canyon, and he had a premonition that was just what was liable to happen if they didn't get out in a hurry. He heaved a sigh of relief when the canyon walls at last fell away and the star-burned prairie rolled before their eyes. Another half hour and they were pounding south on the open trail.

They found Grant Emory, a badly worried Emory, awake when they reached the ranchhouse long after midnight. He greeted them with great relief.

'I figgered mebbe yuh'd decided to stay in town, but I couldn't be sure,' he explained. 'The last thing yuh said before leavin' was that yuh'd sure be back for supper. I was sure gettin' jumpy. What happened?'

They told him; Hatfield spoke in terse sentences, while Sharon stressed the part the Ranger played in the affair. Emory's face blackened with rage as he listened and his hands balled into anger-trembling fists.

'This is gettin' beyond bearin'!' he roared. 'Not even wimmen folks safe any more. Hatfield, I sure owe yuh a heap.'

'I got the breaks,' Hatfield smiled. 'And now I figure the little lady had better hit the hay. She looks sort of peaked.'

After Sharon had retired, Emory strode back and forth nervously, muttering and clenching his fists.

'If it hadn't been for you they would have killed her,' he declared hoarsely.

'I don't know,' Hatfield admitted. 'Killing a woman is going a mite far, even for a bunch like that, but I agree they could hardly have turned her loose.'

'And they would have got away with it,' rumbled Emory. 'Nobody would have suspected 'em. It's easy to figger what folks would have thought—good lookin' cowboy and purty girl ride away together and don't show up no more. Things like that have happened before. I sure hope it don't, though,' he added with a wry smile.

Hatfield chuckled. 'I don't figure you have

123

anything to worry about on that score,' he comforted. 'I've a notion the little lady isn't going to ride away from here with anybody, that is unless you two decide to sell out and pull up stakes.'

'I sure hope not,' Emory repeated, 'but I'm scairt I ain't got much to offer a smart, purty girl like her.'

'Feeling that way gives you plenty to offer,' Hatfield replied.

Emory paused in his pacing, turned to the book shelves and took down a volume.

'I'm too worked up to sleep,' he said. 'Reckon I'll just study a mite.'

Hatfield glanced at the title of the book. It was 'Elementary English Grammar.'

Emory looked up, a trifle sheepishly. 'I'm tryin' to learn to talk a mite better,' he explained. 'I never got a chance for much schoolin'. I was purty young when Dad cashed in, and Mom had it purty hard until she married Wes Remington, years later. I had to go to work early.'

Hatfield nodded. There was a glow in his green eyes and he looked very pleased.

'Many a jigger has gotten a good education all by himself, when he was older than you,' he said. 'So those books over there aren't yours?'

'Hell, no,' denied Emory. 'They might as well be writ in some other language for all I could make head or tail of what's in 'em. They belonged to Wes Remington. He was smart, and eddicated, like Sharon.'

Hatfield nodded again, looking even more pleased.

'Go to it,' he said, patting Emory on the shoulder. 'And have Sharon give you a hand when the going gets tough. I know she'll be glad to and she should be able to help you a lot. By the way, if you don't mind, I'd like to look over those books sometime. They look interesting.'

Emory shook his head enviously. 'Wish they was to me,' he replied. 'Sure, help yourself to 'em any time yuh feel like it. Yuh'll have considerable spare time after the round-up is over.'

CHAPTER ELEVEN

Three days later the round-up started. The south-west range of the Scab Eight, because of its central location relative to the other spreads of the valley, was chosen as the main holding spot. All the cowmen of the valley were present, even Talbot Morrow being driven to the scene in a buckboard so that he might observe the activities, though his condition made it impossible for him to take part in the work.

Walsh Knox had been chosen round-up boss, and he proved an efficient choice. In such an affair, personal animosities and preferences go by the board. Knox immediately appointed Grant Emory his chief lieutenant, it being generally agreed that Emory was about the best top-hand in the valley.

'That is, he used to be,' the cowboys told one another after the first day's work. 'He sure ain't no snide, but he can't twirl his loop within a steer's length of that big feller Hatfield. Gentlemen, there's the sort of cowhand yuh hear tell about and don't ever see. He's even got it all over Walsh Knox, and that's goin' some.'

Knox and Emory handed the cowboys their powders and the hands got busy carrying out the orders. Starting out in groups, each group under the direction of a leader chosen by the round-up boss, they began scouring the range in search of vagrant cattle as well as large bunches. The groups quickly broke up into small parties which soon scattered until each man was covering as much ground as was practicable. Where the ground was rough and broken, careful searching was necessary to gather up small bunches of individual cows. Soon cattle began arriving at the holding spot where they were surrounded and held in close herd. Then began the work of cutting out of the various brands and running the tallied cows to various subsidiary holding spots. Later each owner would cut his own herd, selecting beefs for shipment and running the culls back onto the range. All canyons, coulees, foothills and

126

brakes were carefully combed for strays.

'I don't want any mavericks found strayin' around after this cow hunt is over,' Knox warned his lieutenants who passed on the word to their men.

The southwest range of the Lazy R was the most difficult piece of ground to work. The foothills were slashed with canyons and there were large stands of thick chaparral growth. After the first day's work, Emory shrewdly handed this chore to Hatfield and a group of picked riders.

'And I'll bet a hatful of pesos yuh won't find even a patch of hair on a bush when that big jigger gets through with the section,' Emory boasted to Knox. The Shanghai M foreman grunted, and tugged at his chin whiskers, but did not attempt to argue the point.

'We got a nice shippin' herd, all right,' Emory told Sharon Remington, 'but believe me we lost cows durin' the past coupla months! That herd is just about a third less than what it should be.'

'And we can't afford any such loss, with the obligations the ranch has to meet,' the girl returned in worried tones. 'How did the other spreads pan out?'

'They all lost,' Emory replied, 'but we lost the most. We're on a bad spot, down here next to the desert, of course. Gives the hellions the best whack at us. The only range that showed anythin' what it should have was the southwest range that Hatfield worked.'

'And that range is the closest to the desert,' the girl remarked.

'Uh-huh, it is. Yuh know, Hatfield mentioned that, too, in a funny way.'

'How is that?'

'He said he wasn't surprised, that he figgered that range would make the best showin'.'

'I wonder what he meant by that?'

'I dunno. When I asked him he just smiled, that smile of his what sometimes turns the corners of his mouth down a mite and don't never get up to his eyes like his smiles usually do. That's the second time I saw him smile that way. He did when Jud Hawkins of the Fiddle-Back, who's a bad tempered cuss, hit his horse with his fist for swellin' against the cinch. Hatfield smiled that way at Jud, and said, "Don't do it again, Hawkins."'

'What did Hawkins do?'

'Well, Jud has a rep'tation of bein' a mighty tough hombre, but he took a look at Hatfield's face—them green eyes were like a gun barrel glintin' in the moonlight—and pulled in his horns pronto. He won't hit a horse again, I figger, not when Hatfield's around.'

The evening when the shipping herd was open-corralled on the Lazy R range, Hatfield and Emory found Sheriff Reeves at the ranchhouse when they rode in.

'Just dropped down to see how things were goin',' he said.

'Better figger on spendin' the night,' said Emory. 'It's gettin' ready to rain cats and dogs, or I'm a heap mistook.'

Emory proved a good weather prophet, for by the time supper was over the rain was coming down hard and the night was black as the inside of a bull in fly time. Emory, however, buttoned on his slicker and departed to keep an eye on the night hawks who were guarding the herd. He was taking no chances with that herd. Sharon retired soon afterward and Hatfield and the sheriff were left alone in the big living room.

'Got a letter for yuh,' the sheriff said, drawing an envelope from his pocket. 'It's from Bill McDowell. The outer envelope was addressed to me, like yuh told him to do in that message yuh sent.'

Hatfield opened the letter and spread it on the table. 'We'll read it together,' he said, and bent over the page.

Walsh Knox (Captain Bill wrote) *left Yuma county, Arizona, about six months ago. He accompanied his boss, a man named Talbot Morrow, who was a crippled man, and another cowhand named Quales. It seems Morrow was a very sick man, his legs paralyzed by a bullet that had lodged in his spine and which the doctors were afraid to remove. The doctors gave Morrow less than a year to live, I learned. Morrow was heading back to the Big Bend country in Texas, where he was born, to take over property left him by his dad. Knox, who was his spread foreman in Arizona, and Quales went along to look after him on the trip. Morrow sold his spread in Arizona before leaving for Texas. He was well thought of and liked in the section, I was informed.*

Knox had a reputation of being a first rate cowman and a salty proposition. I learned there were stories saying that he once belonged to a smuggling outfit, also that he ran cows across the Border from Mexico. But it seems nothing was ever proven against him nor any charges brought anywhere so far as the authorities knew.

Of Quales nothing much was known, although it was said he originally hailed from Texas. Knox had worked for Morrow several years. Quales for only a few months. That's about all I was able to get concerning Walsh Knox and his known associates.

'Well,' granted the sheriff, after they had finished the informative portion of the letter, 'it don't tell us much we didn't already know.'

Hatfield, however, sat staring straight ahead of him, his eyes brooding. Suddenly the strangely colored eyes began to glow.

'Sheriff,' he exclaimed, 'mind taking a little ride with me?'

'Anythin' yuh say,' replied Reeves, 'but it's a hell of a night for a ride.'

'And made to order for us,' Hatfield said. 'I've a notion every move I make is being closely watched, but we don't have to worry about anybody tailing us on a night like this. Wait, I'll put the light out, then we'll get into our slickers and slide out the back door.'

Ten minutes later found them riding eastward across the prairie in the driving rain. They reached the Dead Star Trail and turned south. With the plainsman's uncanny instinct for distance and direction, Hatfield divined the spot where the track to the old mine turned from the main trail. With the disgusted sheriff swearing under his mustache, he located, after considerable searching, the stretch of screening brush that hid the entrance to the mine. They pushed their horses through the dripping fringe, halted and listened.

All was dark, however, and there was no sound other than the swishing of the rain and the moan of the wind through the growth. The mine tunnel was silent and deserted. Inside, Hatfield struck a match and lighted a lantern they had brought with them.

The outer rock-walled room was much as he left it the night of his escape from the owlhoots except that the body of Gulden was not in evidence.

'Figured they'd be sure to take him with them,' Hatfield commented. 'I hope they didn't think to take the other one with them and I've a good notion they didn't. It would hardly be

131

recognizeable by now, anyway.'

'What other one? What yuh talkin' about, anyhow?' demanded the puzzled sheriff.

'But without replying, Hatfield led the way to the inner room where he was kept prisoner. The sheriff exclaimed at the mummified corpses of the Indians, but Hatfield did not waste a glance on them. He hurried directly to the corner where lay what looked to be a bundle of rags, but which was the shrunken dessicated body of the man Gulden boasted had worn the prison chain prior to Hatfield, the man who had 'gotten in the Boss's way.'

Nearly all the flesh had sluffed away from the dead man's skull, but the skin of the body remained stretched over the bony skeleton.

Hatfield stripped off the rotting rag that had been a shirt to bare the shrunken chest. Below the ribs on the left side showed the scar of an old bullet wound. He turned the body over on its face. No corresponding scar showed at the back.

Hatfield drew his keen-bladed knife. 'This isn't going to be a nice chore to tackle, but it's necessary,' he told the bewildered sheriff.

With swift, sure strokes he made incisions in the parchment-like skin on either side of the spinal column. He cut away sections of the skin and the withered flesh, and removed several ribs. Suddenly he uttered a sharp exclamation. The sheriff bent close.

'See it?' Hatfield exclaimed, 'stuck in the

132

back-bone?'

'A bullet,' growled the sheriff. 'Uh-huh, a slug, sure as hell.'

'Yes,' Hatfield replied quietly, 'just as I expected. A slug lodged in the backbone, the bullet the doctors were afraid to remove and which paralyzed Talbot Morrow.'

Sheriff Reeves swore luridly. 'And yuh figger this thing here is Tal Morrow?'

'It is,' Hatfield replied.

'Why—why then, that hellion up at the Shanghai M is nothin' but a damned impostor, and a cold-blooded killer along with it!'

'Exactly,' Hatfield said. 'The man posing as Talbot Morrow, the cripple, is Quales, the cowhand who left Arizona with Morrow and Knox.'

Sheriff Reeves leaped erect. 'Come on,' he barked, 'we'll get the blankety-blank. We got him dead to rights. The folks over in Arizona will recognize him as Quales, and not Morrow, right off.'

'Hold it,' Hatfield replied. 'We have very little on him—yet. You could have him sent to prison for perpetrating a fraud, and that's about all. In a comparatively short time he would be out swallerforkin' again and causing trouble for decent folks somewhere.'

'But he cashed in poor Tal Morrow—here's Tal's body to prove it.'

'To prove he is dead, that's all. There is nothing to show that Morrow did not die of

133

natural causes. Remember what Captain Bill's letter said—that the doctor gave Morrow less than a year to live. Quales and Knox would maintain that the trip over here was too much for him and that he died before he got here, and that then they cooked up the scheme to get hold of his inheritance. No, we're not ready to move yet.'

'How yuh goin' to get the real goods on the sidewinder then?' demanded the exasperated sheriff.

'I don't know, yet,' Hatfield replied frankly. 'Let's go. We got a long ride ahead of us.'

The sheriff continued to swear and mutter as they got their horses ready.

'And that hellion fooled everybody in the valley,' he marvelled.

'No reason why he shouldn't,' Hatfield returned. 'The set-up was perfect. Talbot Morrow left this section nearly twenty years ago, when he was little more than a boy. Quales is evidently of his general build and appearance. Ordinarily, somebody might note discrepancies in the resemblance. But the chief thing is—everybody here was expecting a cripple, that was fixed in every mind. A cripple shows up, or what appears to be a cripple, so naturally nobody doubts it is Morrow. Knox was with Morrow a long time in Arizona and doubtless is familiar with details of Morrow's early life and came here with a pretty good general idea as to who lives here and where.

Also it appears Quales originally hailed from Texas, perhaps from the Big Bend country, which would make it still easier for them to carry on the deception. All set? Let's hit the trail.'

CHAPTER TWELVE

Dawn was streaking the clearing sky when they arrived at the Lazy R ranchhouse. The sheriff went to bed to get a few hours of sleep before heading back to town, but Hatfield sat in the living room, thinking. Finally, with a disgusted exclamation, he got up and began examining the technical books on the shelves. Most of them were standard works with which, as an engineer, he was familiar, but the volume entitled 'Prospecting as a Science' was new to him. He took it from the shelf, sat down and began turning the pages.

Something slipped from between the leaves and fluttered to the floor. Hatfield picked it up. It was a yellowed sheet of paper covered with figures and symbols. He glanced at it idly, recognizing it as the solution of a rather complicated equation in higher mathematics beginning 'V equals the square root of P plus the cube root of M.'

$$(V = \sqrt{P} + \sqrt[3]{M}.)$$

He was about to lay the paper aside when a sudden familiarity of the tiny lettering and finely drawn lines struck him. His brows knitted in perplexity. Abruptly he exclaimed aloud, and fumbled with his secret belt pocket. He drew forth the mysterious map and spread it beside the paper.

'I thought so,' he muttered. 'The writing is identical. Whoever worked out this equation also drew the map. And who else but old Weston Remington, Sharon's father! This *is* interesting.'

He stared at the two papers, suddenly noted something that caused him to bend closer, his eyes narrowing.

'Blazes!' he exclaimed. 'What I took for a V on the map isn't a V at all. It's a Radical Sign! That sentence on the map doesn't read—"V of Perdida to Harqua—Perdida W." It reads "The square root of Perdida to Harqua—Perdida W," meaning the square root of the distance from Perdida Peak to Harqua Mine, I'll bet a hatful of pesos. And Perdida W means west from Perdida Peak, I'll bet on that, too. The square root of the distance from Perdida Peak to the Harqua Mine west of Perdida Peak. Let's see, now, I'd estimate the distance from Perdida Peak to the mine as around fifty miles. The square root of fifty is seven, plus. West a little more than seven miles. That would put the point designated well into the mountains over there.'

He stared at the map, exclaimed again.

'And these lines that didn't seem to mean anything. They form a right triangle, with the right angle formed by a line drawn directly south from the Harqua Mine and a line drawn west from Perdida Peak seven miles west and on that line drawn from the Harqua, doubtless, near where the angle is formed. That's what old Remington was trying to show. This is his map, and the key is in the lettering, although if I hadn't happened on this second paper and saw that he made the Radical Sign with an unusually short horizontal bar, I'd have kept on thinking the sign was a V, and getting nowhere. Looks like I'm due for another ride, but not in the daytime. Well, now I can sleep.'

Hatfield was up in time, however, to speak to the sheriff before he rode to town.

'Get set for business,' he told Reeves. 'I've a notion we're going to get the break I hoped for. You'll hear from me soon, if things work out.'

Hatfield was busy with ranch chores all day. He went to bed early, as did the other tired cowboys. But in the dark hours before dawn he slipped out of bed, dressed quietly in the dark and headed for the barn. A few minutes later he was riding swiftly west across the range. Before the break of morning he was in the foothills of the mountains to the west. He worked his way south until he was directly opposite the mighty bulk of Perdida Peak. Then he turned Goldy and headed due west. A mile, two miles he rode, climbing the ragged slopes of the hills. It was full day now. He reined Goldy in as he passed through a thicket and sighted, directly ahead, a towering rock wall fully a thousand feet in height.

Hatfield stared at the tremendous rampart. 'Well,' he told himself, 'there's sure no going west any farther than this, though I figure I've come about the right distance anyhow.'

He rode closer and examined the mighty barrier with the eye of a geologist. He shook his head dubiously. If there was ever rock devoid of mineral content, it was this wall of gloomy granite fanging upward into the blue of the Texas sky.

'But if it doesn't place the line of the long leg of the triangle, I'm making a big mistake in my estimates,' he declared. He saw that the line of cliffs extended south as far as the eye could reach. To the north it apparently ended a little more than a mile from where he forked the sorrel. He turned and gazed across the rangeland to the spire of Perdida.

'A mite south of that hill right now,' he decided. 'Reckon I'd better try north first.'

He rode slowly along the face of the cliff, threading his way among bristles of thicket and clumps of stone. It was difficult and tortuous track along the base of the wall, but possible to negotiate. From time to time he studied the rock as he rode. Suddenly his eyes narrowed with interest.

The upper portion of the wall was changing.

138

Hatfield could see that a lighter colored stone was replacing the basic granite that still formed the foundation of the great natural battlement. The difference in the stone was slight in appearance. It would doubtless have been overlooked by anyone not well grounded in such matters. But the line of cleavage, diagonalling down the wall to the north, was, to the Lone Wolf, plainly apparent.

'A not unusual formation,' he mused. 'During the great volcanic upheavals of millions of years ago, a strata overlying the lower granite was thrust upward by pressure from beneath or by a lateral squeezing force. A dozen such layers show in the walls of the Grand Canyon of the Colorado. That rock up there is plumb different from this lower down, although it looks much the same. If it keeps slanting down this way, before I reach the end of the cliffs, it should be low enough for me to get a good look at it. Sure appears to be quartz, all right. This thing is beginning to tie up after all.'

Another half-mile and he saw that the cliff wall did end, directly ahead. Almost at his feet was the sheer drop of a perpendicular-sided canyon of great depth. The right-angling cliff wall to the west formed the lofty rim-rock of the canyon west of this point. And here the upper strata of lighter colored stone had dropped to almost level with the ground.

'Quartz, all right, not granite,' the Ranger

muttered, staring at the cold, gray surface. 'Well, right around here I should hit on what old Remington was trying to show, or I don't hit on it at all. I'm directly in line west from Perdida Peak now. But I sure don't see anything promising.'

He dismounted and walked to the lip of the canyon, glancing down into its gloomy depths. Far far below, he could see shadowy black fangs of stone and the tops of pine trees looking fragile as feathers at the bottom of the tremendous drop. He leaned over the edge, craned his neck and stared up the western continuation of the great wall. Up and up it soared, its beetling surface shimmering wanly in the morning sunlight, its crest ringed about with saffron flame.

Suddenly Hatfield observed something that quickened his interest. Slanting up the cliff face was what appeared to be a wide ledge that continued until it reached the crest. For a moment he was at a loss to account for such an unexpected formation, then the obvious explanation occurred to him.

'That upper rock is softer than the granite,' he reasoned. 'The granite is in the nature of a great cup holding the quartz formation in its bowl. The quartz is the softer stone and more susceptible to erosion. In the course of untold ages, it has weathered more than the granite and has receded from the base rock, that's all. That ledge is the lip of the broader granite base. And it should extend all the way down and around the corner here.'

Closer examination proved this to be the case. The ledge curved around the angle and descended until it tapered off to a narrow shelf but a few feet above the ground.

Hatfield walked to the beginning of the shelf and peered upward. He could see but a short distance—only to where the ledge curved around a bulge a few yards higher up. He dropped his eyes to the ground and noticed several small fragments of stone lying beneath the shelf. Something in their appearance caught his eye. He stooped and picked one up.

It was cracked and crumbly, and sprinkled through it, thick as raisins in a pudding, were irregular lumps of a dull yellow colour. Also there were crooked yellowish 'wires' criss-crossing the surface of the rock. Hatfield whistled softly as he turned it over in his fingers.

'Exactly the same as the chunk of high-grade I took from that salt cart,' he exclaimed. 'Right here is where that cart-load came from. This is what Weston Remington found. And this is what he was murdered for. That prospector, Avery! Remington must have told him of the find, and not being a practical mining man himself, he was doubtless not quite sure of what he *had* found and brought Avery up here to show him the ledge and get his opinion. Avery killed Remington, and stole his map. He knew, of course, that the ledge was on land owned by Remington and that he couldn't locate the claim himself. All he could do was sneak out loads of high-grade after he had shaved his whiskers and disguised himself. But how did Quales, posing as Talbot Morrow, catch on to it? And how did he know Avery had the map? That was why Avery was killed, of course, to get that map away from him, although I've a prime notion that if Quales had gotten hold of it he wouldn't have been able to decipher the key. Well, I figure to get the answer to those two posers before long. Now to find out just where this stuff came from.'

He scrambled onto the shelf and began climbing the ledge. It was narrow at first, but quickly widened. Also, it slanted inward, like the petal of a flower. Soon Hatfield found himself scrambling upward between the towering face of the cliff on his left, and an upward sloping rim of stone on his right. He realized that he would be invisible to anybody who might happen to be on the ground at or near the base of the cliff. He had covered perhaps a score of yards and was some thirty feet above the ground when he halted abruptly, staring at the face of the cliff. His attention was fixed on a wide, irregular band of darker gray marbled with black and reddish-yellow splotches that furrowed the cliff parallel to the outer wall of the shelf and extended indefinitely upward. He moved forward a few more paces, and paused again.

Here there was a scored-out hollow in the surface of the peculiar looking band, scored out unmistakably by tools wielded by the hand of man. Chisel and drill marks were plain to see against the face of the rock. And the floor of the shelf was littered with stone fragments.

Hatfield exclaimed with satisfaction. He had discovered at last what old Weston Remington had indicated on his cryptic map—the location of a vein of astonishingly rich high-grade gold ore. Here the driver of the salt cart, the pseudo-*peon* who was undoubtedly Avery the prospector, had secured the load of ore that vanished so mysteriously from the Lazy R ranchhouse yard.

'No wonder the hellions wanted to get all that ore away before it could be analyzed by the Harqua Mine people,' Hatfield told himself. 'A careful examination would have showed it wasn't Harqua rock, and soon as the word got around, everybody in this end of Texas would have been pawing over the section trying to locate the ledge. And the chances are that somebody might have hit on it by accident, just like Weston Remington did, although he evidently believed there was metal in these hills.'

He examined the outcropping with great care and quickly became convinced it was no mere pocket of rich ore, but a definite vein of unknown extent and doubtless immense value.

With a sense of intense satisfaction, he sat down with his back against the cliff, fished out the makin's and rolled a cigarette. He consumed the brain tablet with quiet enjoyment, pinched out the butt and rose to his feet. In an endeavour to ascertain the extent of the vein he scrambled up the steep shelf. It wormed and twisted in and out of depressions in the cliff and wound around bulges, so that at no time could he see ahead more than a short distance.

The vein extended for several hundred feet before it finally petered out.

'Plenty of width for easy working, and in depth it may extend for miles down into the earth,' he decided at length. 'Well, it will make a mighty nice wedding present for Emory and the little lady.'

Urged on by curiosity as to what he might find there, he continued to climb the ledge until he reached the crest of the cliff. Finally he scrambled out onto the flat top of the great precipice.

The level surface extended westward for hundreds of yards. Hatfield walked across and stood on the far lip. On this side the contours were different. A fairly steep slope rolled downward to the far-off floor of a wide canyon that bored southward through the hills.

'Opens out onto or west of the desert, the chances are,' Hatfield mused. 'May be a continuation of that canyon up to the north

144

where the owlhoots have their cabin hangout. I wouldn't be surprised if it is, and I wouldn't be surprised, either, if it's the route by which they ran south the cows stolen from the valley. Of course those cows, or most of them, never went south by way of the Dead Star Trail. They were sunk north and hid away in the canyons on the southwest range of the Shanghai M. Then, on dark nights, they would be slid into that crack in the hills and run south over to the west of the desert, where the going is easy enough. Quales, having eased out most of the old Shanghai M waddies and replaced them with his own men, could arrange the chores for his hands so that none of the honest punchers who worked for old Arn Morrow would be used on that southwest range. Simple enough scheme, under the circumstances. Easy to get by with, with nobody having any reason to suspect anything off-color about the Shanghai M set-up. Folks, all thinking that Quales was Talbot Morrow would reason just like Grant Emory did, that it would be impossible for cows to be run north without being seen by the Shanghai M outfit. That's why so few cows were missing from the Lazy R southwest range. Distance was too great to risk a night run to the hole-ups.'

He walked back to the ledge and descended to the ground once more, glanced at the sun, mounted Goldy and rode south. He rode for many miles before he worked his way out of the hills and turned north by east. He was taking no chances with possible observers. Anybody spotting him now would have no reason to suspect where he had actually entered the hills under cover of darkness.

CHAPTER THIRTEEN

When Hatfield reached the Lazy R ranchhouse, late in the afternoon, he was surprised to find Sheriff Reeves impatiently awaiting him. The sheriff was alone in the living room and came to the subject of his visit without delay.

'Well,' he growled, 'I've a mighty good notion them hellions caught on and give us the slip. Morrow, I mean Quales, and Knox hightailed out of the section late yesterday. They drove to the railroad in a buckboard. Knox and another jigger carried Quales onto the evening eastbound train. Knox stayed on the train with him. I heard Morrow, I mean Quales, give out that he was goin' east for an operation that would give him back the use of his legs. Huh! I bet he's usin' 'em right now, puttin' distance between him and this section!'

To the sheriff's surprise, Hatfield did not appear particularly perturbed over what he, Reeves, considered important and disquieting news. He merely nodded and began rolling a cigarette. Sheriff Tom swore an exasperated oath.

'If I'd just got back in town in time yesterday, I'd have dropped a loop on the two sidewinders before they trailed their twine,' he growled.

'Mighty glad you didn't get back in time,' Hatfield remarked.

The sheriff stared, his jaw dropping. 'What—how—' he sputtered.

'If you had arrested Quales and Knox, you would have spoiled everything,' Hatfield interrupted. 'As it is, we have a chance to corral the whole bunch. Things are getting hot, and Quales feels that he must be on the job all the time, not posing as a cripple in his ranchhouse most of it. He and Knox didn't ride that train any great distance. Right now, I'll bet a peso, they are back in this section and ready for business. I figure they're getting mighty jumpy and it will be easy to bait a trap for them.'

In terse sentences he described what he had found in the western hills. The sheriff exclaimed in amazement.

'No wonder they were working every way they knew how to drop a loop on that claim,' he said. 'It'll be worth more than the Harqua, judgin' from what you saw. And now what? Yuh got a plan?'

'Yes,' Hatfield replied, 'I've got one. Here it is, and the chore you have to do. I figure you'll need about ten special deputies you can trust to the limit. Take Emory along and a few of his best hands. They got a right to be in on it. You

147

pick the rest.'

The sheriff listened, tugging his mustache. He shook his head dubiously when Hatfield had finished.

'Son,' he said, 'yuh'll be takin' one awful chance. If something slips, it'll be curtains for you. Baitin' a trap like that with yourself is puttin' yuh in the position of a worm on a hook with a big fish headed his way.'

'Sometimes the worm wiggles off the hook before the fish gets there,' Hatfield smiled.

'Uh-huh,' the sheriff replied dryly, 'and you'd better wiggle mighty peart when the time comes!'

Two days later Hatfield rode away from the Lazy R ranchhouse in the bright sunlight of the early afternoon. He rode at a leisurely pace, lounging carelessly in the saddle, apparently paying little attention to anything, but in fact his keen eyes missed nothing. As he neared the first slopes of the western hills he thought he detected motion on the crest of a wooded rise to his left, but could not be sure. He shrewdly noted, however, that the growth which clothed the rise continued almost unbroken to the beginning of the slopes and extended south almost to where Goldy began climbing the first swell of ground.

At an even, unhurried gait the great sorrel took the slopes. Not until he was less than a quarter of a mile from the canyon and the gold ledge, did he quicken Goldy's gait. He covered the final distance quickly, instantly dismounted and tethered the sorrel within plain view, but well to one side. Then he slipped into the thick growth and waited.

Fifteen minutes or so passed, with only the twittering of the birds and the rustling of the leaves to break the silence. Then to his keen ears came a sound, a soft, muffled sound. The beat of slow moving horses' hoofs some distance away. Quickly it ceased and the silence, disturbed only by the peaceful sounds of nature, resumed. Hatfield stood tense and alert, his gaze fixed on the curve of the narrow open space between cliff and growth, a hundred paces or so distant.

Abruptly, without the least advance notice, a man materialized around the bend, peering, listening. He paused a moment, then slipped forward a few paces, halted again. Another came into view, then another and another, until some eight or nine silent figures were grouped at the curve intently eyeing the terrain ahead. Hatfield, peering through the thin screen of growth, could see that all were masked. It was the Quantrell bunch, the dreaded riders of the Dead Star Trail!

Suddenly one of the masked men pointed to Goldy standing with forward pricked ears. There was an instant clutching of weapons. For a moment no move was made, then a tall and broad man slightly in front gestured toward the ledge which wound up the cliff face. There was a bunching of heads, a turning of eyes in that direction. With one accord the group stole forward, headed for the ledge, guns out and ready. They clumped beneath it, peering and listening.

Like a thunderclap Jim Hatfield's voice rang out—

'In the name of the State of Texas! You are under arrest for robbery and murder!'

All heads jerked toward the sound of his voice. A crashing sounded in the brush that flanked the open space. The owlhoots whirled, and stared into the levelled guns of Sheriff Reeves and his posse.

Hatfield stepped into full view. His face was set in bleak lines. His eyes were coldly gray. On his broad breast gleamed the silver star of the Texas Rangers. His voice rang out again.

'Drop those guns! You're covered!'

There was an instant of paralyzed inaction. Then, with a scream of maniacal fury a tall and slender owlhoot and thrust forward his gun and fired point blank at the Ranger.

But the Lone Wolf weaved sideways in a flicker of movement as the outlaw pressed trigger. His hands flashed down and up. The two reports boomed as one. Hatfield stood tall and erect, but the masked man went down, kicking and clawing among the rocks. The air rocked to the roar of six-shooters.

A posseman pitched forward on his face. Another reeled back, clutching at his blood spouting arm. But the owlhoots were falling fast. Half went down before the possemen's first volley. Another fell. The others flung down their guns and howled for mercy. All except the tall, broad-shouldered leader. He whirled with lightning speed, leaped to the ledge and dived into the shelter of the slanting outer wall, lead spatting the cliff face above his head.

Jim Hatfield raced forward, hurled the hand-lifted owlhoots from his path, leaped over a body on the ground and gained the ledge.

'Wait, Jim, wait!' roared Sheriff Reeves.

'Can't!' Hatfield shot back at him as he vanished into the cleft. 'If he gets to that slope on the west he'll give us the slip!' The possemen heard his boots beating the stony surface of the ledge.

But the outlaw leader had a head start. Twice Hatfield glimpsed him, darting around bulges far to the front. Each time he snapped a shot at the fleeing figure, and each time he knew he had missed. Grimly he set himself to run Quales down before he could reach the cliff crest. Slowly he gained, but now the crest was near, and Quales was still considerably ahead.

On the ground below, the possemen secured their prisoners and began ripping off the masks from the faces of dead and living. Sheriff Reeves and Grant Emory ran east along the slightly curving canyon rimrock until they could see the top of the towering wall and the point where the ledge reached it. Every sense strung to hair-trigger alertness they waited. They heard Hatfield's shots, muttered under their breath, clutched their own weapons, never taking their eyes from the summit of the great wall.

Suddenly a tiny figure leaped into view on the cliff top, ran a few steps along the edge and whirled. A second figure appeared. Emory and Reeves could see the spurts of smoke and hear the thin crack of the guns as the two figures dodged and circled. Quickly they vanished from sight. A last stutter of shots drifted down to the watching pair.

Abruptly one of the figures reappeared, reeling back and back toward the cliff edge. It slumped, staggered another step and fell plummetlike from the dizzy verge. Turning slowly in the air it rushed downward and vanished into the gloomy depths of the canyon.

The second figure came into view, leaned over the lip, stared into the canyon. Then it turned and walked west and vanished.

Sheriff Reeves, his features set like granite, turned to the white-faced Emory.

'Well,' he said in a husky voice that quivered with emotion, 'the hellion got away. That was poor Jim went into the cabin. Quales bested him and hightailed west for the slope. Come on, let's see about the rest of those sidewinders.'

Four of the owlhoots were dead. Three, one wounded, were still erect and firmly secured. Walsh Knox lay on the ground, breathing in hoarse gasps. A quick examination told the sheriff he was mortally wounded and going fast. The sheriff was about to give orders toward the disposition of the prisoners when a scuffling sound came from the ledge above his head. He looked up quickly, saw the dimpled crown of a hat showing above the outer wall. Another instant and he gave a joyous yell.

'Hatfield!' he whooped. 'We figgered yuh to be done for sure when we saw yuh turn and walk west!'

'Quales dropped his gun when I drilled him,' Hatfield replied, slipping from the ledge to the ground. 'I went back to pick it up. Souvenir. Sorry I gave you a start.'

He walked over to where Knox lay and gazed down at the dying man. Knox's lips quirked slightly in the ghost of a smile. He beckoned feebly. Hatfield bent close.

'Feller,' panted Knox, 'here's a chance to even up for them matches and tobacco I give yuh that night in the mine. I want yuh to do somethin' for me.'

'I'll do anything I can for you, Knox,' Hatfield promised compassionately.

'Tell Sharon,' whispered the dying man, 'tell Sharon goodbye for me. Tell her I wish I'd always rode a straight trail like Grant Emory.

Then mebbe I'd had a chance with her. Emory and me fell out over her, yuh know.'

'I'll tell her,' Hatfield promised. 'I've a notion she'll be glad to hear yuh went out thinking of her and making a wish like that.' He hesitated, gazing at Knox's contorted face.

'Tell me something, Knox,' he said. 'Avery, the prospector was one of Quales' outfit, wasn't he?'

'Yes,' panted Knox. 'He double-crossed us. Weston Remington used to come up to the *casa* to talk with Quales, who he thought was Tal Morrow, the son of his old friend. He showed Quales a chunk of the ore and Quales found out somehow he'd made a map of the claim and meant to give it to Sharon. Quales knew the strike was worth a fortune, but Remington wasn't sure of what he had—thought mebbe it might be just a shallow pocket, and he hadn't finished getting title to the hill land. He kept the location under his hat. Quales set Avery to get in with him and find out what Remington knew. Avery looked to be an honest old timer with his gray hair and whiskers and Remington trusted him. He took Avery to the claim to get his opinion on it. Avery cashed in Remington and got his map. But he didn't come back to Quales. He hightailed out of the section. But he come back, after he'd shaved his whiskers and dyed his hair. Quales was almighty smart and spotted him right off. He set the boys to tail him. Avery was slippery and the boys couldn't catch him up. Quales knew he was slippin' out high-grade ore and sellin' it below the Border. He set a trap for him down by Perdida Peak, knowin' he had to use the Dead Star Trail to get across the desert. You know how that ended.'

Knox's eyes closed, but opened almost immediately. 'Uh-huh,' he whispered, 'and I'm ended, too. Ended like a jigger what rides a crooked trail always ends.'

The eyes closed wearily once more. They did not open again.

*   *   *

As they rode out of the hills, with the possemen herding the prisoners ahead and assisting their own two wounded members, Grant Emory asked Hatfield a question—

'Jim, what made yuh first suspect Quales?'

'Mud,' the Lone Wolf smiled and replied, 'mud on the inner sides of his boot-heels.'

'Huh?'

'Remember the afternoon we rode up to the Shanghai M *casa* to discuss details of the round-up? Recall I was sitting on the edge of the porch. Quales, posing as Talbot Morrow, the cripple, was sitting in a chair. From where I sat I had a good view of the inner sides of the high heels of his riding boots. The inner sides of the heels were caked with fresh mud. Now Morrow was supposed to be a cripple who couldn't stand on his feet. It looked mighty funny for a man who couldn't walk to have fresh mud on the heels of his boots. It sure set me to wondering. His hands helped, too.'

'How's that?' asked the sheriff.

'They were strong, virile hands, deeply tanned,' Hatfield replied. 'Not the sort of hands you'd expect a man to have who'd spent the past two years inside, as Morrow was said to have done. That looked mighty funny, too. And right about then I was looking hard for somebody who might be Quantrell, the owlhoot. I'd already eliminated Emory here as a suspect.'

'Yuh sort of suspected me at first, then?' said Emory.

'Yes,' Hatfield answered. 'You see, that morning when I wounded two of the bunch down by Perdida Peak, you showed up at the ranchhouse a little later, riding out of the desert, with two of your men bullet punctured. Set me to thinking, all right, but it didn't take long to get you in the clear.'

'How?'

Hatfield paused to roll and light a cigarette.

'Because,' he said, 'it didn't take me long to arrive at the conclusion that you were a man of very little education.'

'What did that have to do with it?' asked the sheriff.

Before replying, Hatfield fumbled a bit of greasy paper from his belt pocket.

'I received this note just before I rode to the Perdida section,' he said. 'It was a loco looking thing to which I attached little importance and I was about to destroy it when I noticed something funny about it. See this wording? It reads: "You aint got a chance in an hundred to git out alive." Well, the note appeared to be an illiterate scrawl, but no illiterate would ever use that construction *"an* hundred" instead of *"a* hundred." Only a man of considerable education would use the indefinite article *an* that way. Right there the writer of the note slipped a mite. Didn't seem much, but it meant considerable to Emory, the way things turned out, and saved me wasting time trying to get something on an innocent jigger. So, as I said, I was on the lookout for somebody who might be Quantrell. I'd already tied up Walsh Knox as one of the Quantrell bunch.'

'How?' asked Emory.

'The night they had me corralled in the old mine, that forward jutting chin whisker of Knox's showed plain under his mask. Also, Knox had a habit of pulling at his beard. He raised his hand to do it twice while he was talking to me. He went to fetch the boss of the outfit, who, of course, was Morrow, or rather Quales. But until I got Captain Bill's letter, I was badly puzzled just the same, for it seemed just about certain that Talbot Morrow *was* a cripple and had been for a couple of years. It was not reasonable he would have started building up such a pose two years beforehand. But Captain Bill's letter made everything plumb plain. Three men left Arizona together. Only two showed up in Texas. Right then I was sure the supposed-to-be Morrow was Quales. And you know what we found in the mine, Sheriff.'

'Uh-huh, poor Tal Morrow's body,' nodded Reeves. Suddenly he chuckled.

'I was sure lookin' sideways at Emory when he come into the saloon at Gavilan all scratched up that night of the row in the mine office and them two hellions went through the window,' he confessed.

Hatfield smiled. 'I eliminated Emory of taking part in that chore the next morning,' he remarked. 'I questioned the mine super about the two hellions he got a look at. He told me their masks were tied tight over their faces. A jigger with his face wrapped up in a cloth would hardly get scratched much going through a window.'

The sheriff shook his head in admiration. 'You sure don't miss a trick,' he exclaimed.

'That attempted payroll robbery on the trail between Gavilan and Dorantes helped tie things up with Morrow, too,' Hatfield added. 'It showed that somebody in the Quantrell outfit had means of learning considerable about the Harqua Mine Company's business. And I'd already learned that Quales, as Morrow, owned some stock in the Harqua and was chummy with the superintendent.'

'You figured that salt cart driver was Avery, the prospector?' asked Emory.

'Yes, after Sharon told me the story of her father's death. The jigger who was driving the cart had his hair dyed black and had recently shaved off a heavy beard he had been wearing for years. And I figured Avery to be the only man other than Remington who knew where that high-grade ore was coming from. I'd already decided it didn't come from the Harqua mine. The hellions were too desperately anxious to prevent a specimen being given a close examination. Avery would dig out a cart load of the ore, slip across the valley at night with the ore covered with a layer of salt and then amble down to Mexico as a salt peddler, and nobody who happened to see him would think anything of him or his load.'

'And Quales figgered to get hold of the Lazy R,' remarked Emory.

'Yes, in one way or another. I've a notion it was Knox saved your hide for you. Knox had a streak of decency in him and I figure he wouldn't stand for having you dry-gulched, because you had once been friends and he knew Sharon liked you. Of course, Quales was the brains and the boss of the bunch, but he knew better than to push Knox too far. So he contented himself with systematically cleaning the Lazy R of cows, knowing that if you kept on losing, you would be unable to meet your bank

159

obligations and have to go out of business. Then, of course, he would buy up the Lazy R and the gold ledge with it. The only flaw in his scheme was that he didn't know where the ledge was. That's why I figured we could trap him as we did today. He was sure I got the map from Avery and did know where the ledge was, and he figured I'd lead him to it. Well, I did, but it didn't do him much good.'

'Reckon he's makin' a lunch for the coyotes down in that canyon tonight,' grunted the sheriff. 'Betcha he pizens 'em.'

The sheriff rode on to town with his prisoners. Hatfield elected to spend the night at the Lazy R.

'Sorry I can't stay for the wedding,' he told Sharon the following morning, 'but Captain Bill will have another little chore ready for me by the time I get back to the post. So I'll just kiss the bride *before* the ceremony, and be riding!'

We hope you have enjoyed this Large Print book. Other Chivers Press or G.K. Hall & Co. Large Print books are available at your library or directly from the publishers.

For more information about current and forthcoming titles, please call or write, without obligation, to:

Chivers Press Limited
Windsor Bridge Road
Bath BA2 3AX
England
Tel. (01225) 335336

OR

G.K. Hall & Co.
P.O. Box 159
Thorndike, Maine 04986
USA
Tel. (800) 223-2336

All our Large Print titles are designed for easy reading, and all our books are made to last.